S0-DGB-872

SOJOURNERS

10/04

For Niell.

Thanks for the
inspiration!

Dale Howard

SOJOURNERS

A
Tale
of
TRUTH

Dale Howard

iUniverse, Inc.
New York Lincoln Shanghai

SOJOURNERS
A Tale of TRUTH

All Rights Reserved © 2004 by Dale Howard

No part of this book may be reproduced or transmitted in any form
or by any means, graphic, electronic, or mechanical, including
photocopying, recording, taping, or by any information storage
retrieval system, without the written permission of the publisher.

iUniverse, Inc.

For information address:
iUniverse, Inc.
2021 Pine Lake Road, Suite 100
Lincoln, NE 68512
www.iuniverse.com

ISBN: 0-595-32457-6

Printed in the United States of America

There is so much I want to tell you but you can't understand it now. When the Spirit comes, it shall guide you to all Truth.

—John 16:12-13

ACKNOWLEDGEMENTS

It would never be possible to acknowledge all the creative, spiritual, and supportive influences that indirectly shaped this story in one way or another. I can, however, recognize those whose direct contribution had a significant impact on the writer and/or the successful completion of the project.

Marlys Millhiser awakened the creative impulse and introduced the possibility. My wife Darlene has lived through it all with insightful comments and unfailing love. My son Jeff's observations prompted significant improvements to the manuscript. Reverend Tom Catlin's spiritual guidance helped keep me on track. John and Jan Price's much needed support and advice pointed me in the right direction. And, you would not be reading this without the efforts of the folks at iUniverse who provide a respected alternative to the restricted world of traditional publishing.

ONE

The day didn't start out the way I planned. I was supposed to take Pop into town first thing after breakfast. It was two years since the stroke took half of his body and some of his mind. He was pretty bad at first, couldn't even scratch his nose. A month with the physical therapists grinding on him every day got him able to feed and toilet himself, but he still needs watching most of the time. What with physical therapy twice a week, doctor appointments, fifteen different medicines to keep track of, Medicare and social security hassles, wheelchairs that aren't right, hospital beds that don't work, and on and on, I've come to understand what grandma meant when she said, "Old age ain't for sissies". I've sometimes thought it might be better if his spirit had followed where the best part of his mind went after the stroke. I guess it wasn't time for that, yet.

Anyway, life was going its own way this day, not paying any attention to what I thought was important. So, instead of getting Pop ready for town, I was back down at the barn. Kate had decided to drop her calf today. I'd put her in a stall yesterday when I noticed her hipbones had started to sag. It's hard to guess with a first calf heifer and I wasn't taking any chances. Sure enough, this morning Kate was down on her side, straining like her eyes were gonna pop out, and grunting like a pig in a wallow. Her head came up and followed me around when I went down behind her to see what was going on. I didn't like what I saw—two tiny, ivory hooves were all that showed in the swollen opening, but that was enough to tell me this calf was trying to back into the world, and that's the hard way for all concerned. I guess there are worse things than a breech calf in a fear-crazed heifer that's down on her side in a sea of manure, but right then I couldn't think of any.

I headed back to the house to call Doc Johnson, thinking about the curves life likes to toss our way every so often to see if we've still got our priorities straight. Sometimes, though, it seems like the curves turn to fast balls headed right between your eyes, and they're on you before you have time to duck. Most of the time I can remember to remind myself that what's going on in this adventure we call life doesn't matter nearly as much as my human mind wants me to think. But sometimes I forget.

Kate and I are good friends. She's a doe-eyed little Guernsey I found in a ditch two years ago. I never did figure out what a new-born dairy calf was doing in the ditch along side a ranch road in the middle of open range beef country, but I guess we don't need to know everything. She would have been coyote bait for sure if I hadn't happened along.

Kate always had a wistful, melancholy air about her, even when she was little, like she'd lost part of herself somewhere but couldn't quite remember what it was. I expect most of us know what it's like to feel so lost and alone you hope tomorrow won't come. Most people think animals don't have a soul. That's because they don't know any better. It's clear to me that we're all made of the same stuff, some are just more aware of it than others.

I'd often thought what Kate needed was a soul mate and it looked like one was on its way, but it wasn't going to come easy. She's on the small side, even for a Guernsey, and I should have held off breeding her for another six months or so. But a compassionate heart can turn a deaf ear to messages from a practical brain. Sometimes the brain turns out to be right. Even when I manage to remember this warning, I usually go with the heart anyway.

"Can't help you this time, Tom." Even through the phone I could hear Doc's painful breathing. "I've got three busted ribs from dehorning a bunch of crazy range steers. You might try Grady King over at Cottonwood but I doubt he could get there in time to save a breech calf. Best chance is if you get after it yourself." Then he proceeded to give his canned obstetrics lecture. "There's a troublesome place in the birth canal," Doc said with just a hint of impatience, "Where the tube of vagina drops over the pelvic bone and balloons out into a pregnant uterus the size of a medicine ball. The pelvis is like a big boulder right in the middle of the path and sometimes thwarts even a mature cow with a calf that's taking the regular way out. But in a heifer that's trying to back a baby into the world, it can be a fatal obstacle...."

Kate had given up straining by the time I got back to the barn with soap and water. She just lay there on her side, eyes bugged out, taking air in big gulps like she'd never catch up on all she'd breathed out. I threw some bedding down to cover the slop, then stripped off my shirt, scrubbed my arm and lathered it up from fingernails to arm pit. I knelt down behind her and slid my hand inside the swollen opening.

Doc's words ran through my brain as I slowly worked my fingers up one furry leg and found the hips locked up tight at the edge of the pelvis, just like he predicted. With the rest of the little guy dangling off into the abyss below, it didn't look good. My fingers back tracked to the point of the hock and dropped into the groove just below the joint. I gave it a good pinch. And got an indignant jerk for my trouble. Kate might have given up on this baby, but it wasn't ready to quit.

I backed my arm out, and got two strands of bailing twine, like Doc said. Then went back into the bruised vagina and worked the twine up over both hocks. Doc said the hips might break loose if I could twist the calf so it was on its side. So I stood up, wrapped both strings of twine around my wrists and laid into it, cranking on those little legs and pulling for all I was worth. It was like trying to pull a house off its foundation. Nothing moved.

I had to stop. My lungs ached and little white stars swam around my face. I flopped down in the muck and lay over on Kate's thick neck, panting for air to slow my pounding heart. We lay like that for a time, sharing each other's warmth. After a while I reached out to stroke her silky cheek. Her ear twitched a couple of times like she was swatting at flies. Slowly she raised her head and turned toward me. Our eyes locked.

Minutes passed. Then Kate's neck started to tremble, like a cornered rabbit. I jumped behind her and grabbed the loops of twine that disappeared inside. Kate's legs went stiff and a shudder went through her like a tornado plowing ground. I stood up and gave those pulls all I had. The baby's legs moved a couple of inches. I slacked off to take a breath. But Kate wasn't resting. She bore down again, harder this time. A black tail tip appeared between the baby's legs. I lunged for the tail and hung on as Kate let out a bellow that rattled the stanchions. Everything gave at once. I crashed to the floor still holding tight to the twine and the tail. My head bounced off the concrete, and for a minute I couldn't tell day from night. Then my lights blew out, and I went spiraling into a funnel as black as a barrel of tar.

Slowly, the blackness softened, like stage lights coming up on a dawning scene. A dream began to form, swirling out from a gray mist. Even before the mists cleared I knew where the dream had carried me, because the memory I was seeing is so etched into my spirit that it's more real than the face I see every day in the mirror.

I was truly there, in the summer of 1978, seventeen years old and feeling the excitement of strange new places, inhaling intoxicating mountain air laced with cedar and sage, dizzy with the infinite hope of new friends and new beginnings.

Then as sudden as a slap in the face, I was yanked back to the earthy smells of an Arizona barn. I sat up and looked at Kate, my ears clanging. She had rolled onto her chest and was pushing against my arm with a warm, wet nose. I turned. On the straw beside me was a beautiful black baby, glistening with mucous and pieces of membrane. Little clouds of steam rose from the still body, but she wasn't breathing. I felt for her heart. It thudded softly against my fingers. I grabbed a handful of bedding and swabbed out her mouth and nose. Then I picked her up by her hind legs, shook her as hard as I could and swung her back and forth in a big arc like the pendulum on grandpa's old clock.

She coughed. I shook her again like a bulldog hanging onto a pant leg. She coughed again, and took a breath. Then another cough, and another breath. A couple more coughs and she took off breathing like she intended to stay.

I put her down in front of Kate. She looked the baby over good, moaned deep in her chest, and set to work. After a few licks with that rough, gray tongue, the little black face came up and liquid, brown eyes locked on mama.

"Bahhhhh," went the baby.

"Ummm," Kate answered.

With the excitement over, my banging head took charge and forced me back to the floor. I sat for a time, letting my head ease back to tolerable. When I could stand again, I cleaned up the mess and started for the house.

The morning was so clear that the San Francisco Peaks looked near enough to walk to, rather than eighty miles away. A family of top-knotted quail skittered across the path and into the brush.

By the time I got to the house my head was almost back to normal. My wife had breakfast on the table. She was less pregnant than Kate but getting bigger by the week. Pop, in his wheelchair, was pushed up to his usual end of the table, chasing scrambled eggs around his plate with the one arm that still sort of worked.

"We've got a new black baby down at the barn," I announced.

My wife slid me the smile that was reserved just for me. We don't need a lot of words. We have other ways, a look, a touch, a little smile.

"Trouble?" she said. "You look like you fell in a honey wagon."

"Some, but everything's fine now. Kate took to her right away."

"Another miracle," she said, her eyes shining.

"After breakfast we'll roll you down to see her," I said to Pop.

Pop was fiercely concentrating on a spoonful of eggs he had just lifted off his plate. His wobbly arm stopped and the good side of his mouth bowed in a crooked smile, the bad side drooped even lower, ropy saliva drooling from slack lips.

My wife bent over, wrapped her arms around Pop's neck and kissed the bald spot on top of his head. Then she turned to look at me. It was her time to be on the receiving end of a silent message.

Love you, I sent her.

Love you, came right back.

TWO

My mother's name was Ada. I never knew her, but Pop told me all about her when I was old enough to understand. Pop was hard-pressed to say anything bad about anybody, especially my mother, but reading between the lines I came to believe she had half the boys in Chaney County chasing after her like a pack of heat-crazed hounds. Pop would never admit that he knew who finally treed Ada and planted the seed that sprouted into yours truly.

In 1960, an unmarried girl who got herself in a family way was enough of an outrage to send the bible thumpers into apoplexy. But apparently that didn't faze Ada. Pop said she paraded across the stage at her high school graduation looking like there was a watermelon under her blue gown. That sent the courthouse loafers into a holier-than-thou frenzy, and their women's tongues to slashing like the slicer at Holsum Market.

I guess eventually even Ada couldn't stand up under such a vicious assault. I was three weeks old that fall when she bundled me into a peck basket and dumped me on the steps of St. Aidan's parsonage where Pop was the pastor. He took me in, gave me his name, and that's how I grew up, an accidental ward of the Episcopal Church, liberally dosed with equal parts catechism and Pop's original brand of spiritual wisdom.

It took me a long time to understand that Ada did me a great service when she took off. It was bad enough she bore a bastard child with no father, which in time I could hope to live down. But she also tagged me with a name I would carry for the rest of my life. I'd rather she hadn't left me anything. Royal T. (for Thomas), together with Pop's name of Ripley was the chain that bound me for any half-wit to jerk on whenever they felt like it. I tried to get by with Tom when I started to school but I guess the Royal T. was too much to resist.

I suppose it was a combination of my ancestry and my name, but I spent a lot of time alone; most of it, aside from school, working and playing around a ten acre place Pop kept as a refuge outside of town. Pop said I always had a gift with animals, and I guess I do. I do know I grew up appreciating the company of my horse, Skeeter, more than most people I came across.

My name continued to cause me a whole lot of grief until the spring of 1978. It was my junior year of high school and I was seventeen. Pop came into my room where I was struggling with geometry and announced he was retiring after thirty-six years with the church, and we were moving to Arizona. I'd known for some time that his small town congregation wasn't happy with Pop's increasingly maverick views, but I never thought he'd chuck it all and take us off to a brand new life. It was the best news I could ever remember.

By the time school let out we had sold our place and most of our junk. May 28th we loaded up an old trailer with Skeeter, and the rest of our stuff, and headed west. I wasn't sorry to leave Missouri in our dust.

We settled in on a twenty acre ranch, two miles west of the little town of Verde Mesa, about half-way between Phoenix and Flagstaff. I took to Arizona right away. The old house on our place wasn't much to brag about, but we had a sweet-water spring that put out enough to irrigate a good size garden. And, there was a pretty fair barn and corral set up plus some open meadow grazing for stock. The rest of our world for as far as the eye could see was a green carpet of giant ponderosa pines, broken up by islands of paler chaparral that swelled into the snowcapped San Francisco Peaks above Flagstaff, some eighty hazy miles north. Over all this hung a sky so pure it could make your knees buckle.

Before long, besides Skeeter, we had an ole tomcat that came with the place, a Guernsey cow I called Ginger, and Mike, a yellow dog. Right away, Pop lucked into the librarian's job in town, so it was up to me to get the place in shape and put in a garden in the big lot out behind the house.

I guess you could say it was the garden more than anything else which changed my life forever that summer. By the middle of August we had more sweet corn and tomatoes than Pop and I could handle. So, we decided to go into the produce business. One Sunday Pop helped me rig a little cart to hook on behind Skeeter, and Monday afternoon I headed for town to try my luck as a truck garden huckster.

The business took off right away. Most of the housewives were glad to see me with my produce wagon. One lady even gave me a nickel tip on top of the fifty cents for a dozen ears of corn and five big tomatoes. By two o'clock I had worked my way up Granite Street, crossed the town square, down Elm past Veteran's Park, almost emptied the wagon, had nearly five dollars jingling in my pocket, and was looking for shelter.

Since July I'd learned you don't get much warning when a high country summer sky decides to turn on you. In a span of maybe five minutes you can go from dazzling clear to Niagara Falls. Already, dynamite blasts were ripping the skies, and it was certain a frog strangler was ready to cut loose.

I kicked Skeeter into a trot, thinking to head for a canopy of cottonwoods where the street narrowed and became a dirt road that meandered off into a big yellow meadow. Giant globs of angry water slapped at my hat and splattered the dust in the road as we raced past a fading two-story house that sat angled toward the end of the street. Just the other side of the house I spied an overgrown driveway that led up to an old barn maybe a hundred yards behind the house. I thought better of the cottonwoods, yanked Skeeter around, and we beat it fast as we could up the rough drive toward the beckoning barn, the wagon crashing along behind us. The dam in the sky broke as we tore through the barn's wide doorway and skidded to a stop in a cloud of moldy dust.

I rolled off Skeeter's back and shook the rain off my hat. Outside, the storm pounded and raged. I was feeling pretty smug and dry when I heard a low creaking sound start up overhead. I looked up thinking the old barn had weathered one too many storms. A trapdoor in the loft floor directly above my head slowly screeched open, like fingernails drawn across a blackboard. A sliver of light in the opening grew to a pale yellow square as the screeching pitched higher and then stopped.

A head appeared in the trapdoor opening, backlit by the light from behind so the face was in shadow.

"Who goes there?" The head said. A girl.

Another head appeared beside the first one. "And what are you doing in our barn?" A boy.

"I just ducked in out of the storm," I said.

"Well, you can just duck right out again," said the boy head.

"Sure, soon as the rain stops," I said.

"It's nearly stopped," he said.

He was right. The sky still boiled and the roof still dripped, but the raging torrent had slowed to a gentle drizzle.

The alleyway in front of me was blocked by a big double door. I took hold of Skeeter's bridle to back him out through the doorway we came in. Backing up with the wagon behind spooked him, and he froze.

"Do those other doors open?" I asked the heads above me.

"Can't get your horse to back up?" said the boy.

"It makes him nervous," I said.

"No wonder, with a contraption like that behind him," he said.

"The latch is tricky," said the girl. "You have to know how. Just a second, I'll come down and do it."

The heads disappeared for a moment then a wooden ladder scraped through the trapdoor opening. The girl scampered down the ladder face forward, skipping the last three rungs to land lightly on the balls of her feet.

I can still feel the effect of that first electric impression. I'd never spent much time mooning around over girls, and no time imagining the girl of my dreams. But when I saw those bright emerald eyes looking up at me, creamy face framed by thick copper hair held in place by a white ribbon, my knees went loose and I had to remind myself to breathe.

She turned and looked up to the opening overhead. "You coming down?" she said. I guessed her to be about a year younger than me.

The boy's shadow hung over the edge of the opening. "No," he said.

She shrugged and turned toward the closed doors. It took some fiddling with the heavy door latch before it clicked and the doors swung open.

I took hold of Skeeter's bridle and started forward. As we passed a closed stall door, his head went up, his nostrils flared, and he let go a high whuffling sound like he does when kindred spirits are about. A kindred spirit answered back from behind the closed stall door.

"Your horse?" I said to the copper haired girl.

She shook her head. "He's just staying here until they can figure out what to do with him. He threw his owner off and broke his arm."

"Can I have a look?" I said.

"I guess so, if you stay out of reach. He likes to bite, too."

She swung open the top half of the stall door and stepped back. I peeked in. A sleek, chocolate Arabian hugged the far wall, ears laid back, frantic eyes fixed on mine. His fear was a searing, sharp point that shot the distance between us and ran down the length of my spine, leaving my legs wobbling.

"He'll hurt you if he can." This time the boy's voice came from the hallway behind me. "They say he was born mean."

I turned to get a look at him, but he stepped back and blended with the shadows along the wall.

"Animals aren't born mean," I said. "He's just scared."

"He might change your mind if he gets the chance," the boy said from the shadows.

"What's his name," I said.

"Diablo," the gorgeous girl said. "And you better believe the name fits."

I led Skeeter away from the doorway, rummaged in my pocket for an ever present piece of hard candy, and sauntered back to the stall.

I opened the lower half of the stall door. The two kids were still as mice as I peered inside into the gloom. Pop says, rock, plant, man or animal, we're all part of the same universal energy. He says the problem is most of us don't know who we are, where we came from or what we're doing here. And for a soul that feels like it's all alone in the world, sometimes that can be a recipe for paralyzing fear. Even at seventeen I understood that fear is more contagious than the flu, and causes all manner of devilish behaviors. But once you get wise to the spiritual being you really are, it gets easier to ignore the fearful demons your brain conjures up from time to time.

Very early in life I learned that no matter what you're heading into, if you can just remember to remember who you truly are, whatever you face loses most of its scare power, and the roughest path tends to smooth out a good deal.

So, I stuffed away my fears outside the stall, held out my piece of candy, and eased toward the terrified spirit in front of me which, at the moment, happened to be cloaked in eight-hundred pounds of glossy, quivering horseflesh.

"Diablo, the devil horse," I crooned to him.

He looked at me like Marie Antoinette must have eyed the guillotine. I kept easing forward, whispering his name, while he bunched deeper into the corner. I stopped and stood perfectly still, offering the piece of candy on my palm, smiling and sending silent peace signals into the panicked pupil of his bulging eye.

Our eyes locked. Our energies met in the middle of the dim stall, one offering peace, the other a loaded cannon. Minutes passed. Both of us stood our ground.

Then slowly, like a cloud passing over the moon, his eyes began to soften. In a moment, the trembling chest stilled, then the tensed neck relaxed, the ears came forward. I drifted closer. A sudden spasm started at his downy nose, spread up his face, erupted down his neck and shot through his body. The spasm passed. His head bobbed twice, then came around to face me straight on. He stretched the full length of his neck and took a tentative step toward my outstretched hand.

I could hear both kids breathing behind me, at the edge of the stall door. I eased forward. The horse nickered and moved closer. I reached out and lightly ran a finger down his smooth neck. His eyes were clear and easy now, the demon at rest. He lowered his head and nuzzled the candy from my hand.

"I'm impressed," the girl said. A small smile licked at the corners of her mouth.

The boy stepped from the shadows. He looked to be about my age. His hair was long over his ears and silky black, his skin like rich nutmeg, his eyes glistening brown velvet around onyx pupils. He cocked his head to one side and searched my face for the briefest minute, apparently didn't care for what he saw, and turned away back down the alley. I was dismissed.

"Maybe I better be going," I blurted. But I hadn't noticed the rain had started up again. In a blink it was pounding down on the roof like God's personal shower.

"Better wait awhile," the girl said. She turned away toward the ladder. In a moment she stood framed in the trapdoor opening. "Please understand," she said. "It's not that we don't like you. We're just............private."

I wanted to ask what she meant. But before I got started the trap-door screeched shut. After a few minutes the rain stopped and Skeeter and I took our leave.

Those kids were like a powerful magnet, pulling at me even as I took off in the opposite direction, but they plainly didn't share the attraction. I was feeling a little deflated on the way back to the ranch. I had to keep reminding myself that Pop says first impressions are like coffee, the first taste may not set so well on your tongue, but later on you wonder why in the world you thought it was bitter. I decided to give it another try tomorrow.

Then it was time to put the afternoon aside, get Skeeter unhitched and the wagon put away, tend to the livestock, and get supper started before Pop got home from the library. Life on our little Arizona ranch didn't leave much time for mooning around.

THREE

I finally got Pop loaded up, kissed my wife goodbye, and we headed for the physical therapist. I have a heap of respect for PT's. They brought me a long way back after some serious damage several years ago. Pop's twice a week sessions didn't seem to be working any miracles for him, though. Still, every Tuesday and Thursday we go back and they work him over again, everybody hoping for a miracle but really just fighting a holding action. CVA they call it, cerebrovascular accident, doctor-speak for a despicable ambush on an excellent brain that was peacefully going about its miraculous business only a minute before.

I have to keep reminding myself that what happened to Pop is just another adventure into the human condition. One day he'll wake up back where he came from and think *Wow, what a ride that was.* The hard part sometimes is remembering how alive he was before a tiny rogue blood clot laid him low.

So, yet another Tuesday I wait while the PT's wage their futile battle against Pop's inert flesh. With nothing to do but let my mind drift, pretty soon I'm daydreaming. And the dream that clamors for attention is my favorite. With the memories comes a pleasant warmth. I'm seventeen again, and back with two compelling kids in a barn loft. I guess you could say that was the most significant time in my life so far. It certainly is the most finely etched.

I was so fascinated with those strange kids that I had trouble keeping my mind on my business. I kept thinking they must've had a bad experience with some of the town kids, and if I tried again, they might warm up to me.

The next morning dragged. There was a standing rule on the ranch. No matter what else we chafed to be doing, work came first. For me that translated into six mornings each week doing what had to be done that day, and if there was time left over, making progress on some new project. So, after Pop left, I dragged through the morning routine of cleaning up the kitchen, making the beds, and tending the garden. But as soon as lunch was over I was on my bike and racing for Elm Street.

I skidded into the old barn behind their house and stood on a feed bunk rail to thump on the trapdoor to the loft. I used the excuse that I came to see how Diablo, the devil horse, was doing.

They didn't fall over with excitement but didn't try to run me off, and came sliding down the ladder. I tried not to stare like a country rube, but it was hard. The girl was dressed in faded Levi's and a pink T-shirt, and making them both look really good. I didn't notice what the boy had on.

The top half of Diablo's stall door was open and I peered in to see how he was today. He was pressed up against the back wall casting a wary eye in our direction, but not frantic like yesterday. I whispered his name as I leaned over the half door and held out some apple I'd stashed in my pocket. He cocked his head a little to one side and his eyes softened. After a minute he took a step forward, stopped, bobbed once, then sauntered over.

We met in the middle of the stall. I put out a hand and stroked the black velvet of his nose. With the other hand I grabbed a fistful of dark mane and began to back up, urging him through the open door.

The two kids had retreated down the alleyway as we moved past the overhanging eaves of the barn and out into the clearing beyond. I stopped him there. He stood quietly waiting while I moved around and slowly eased up onto his back.

We sat for a moment, getting the feel of each other, sharing the power that flowed between us. I patted his neck and he began to walk, a little mincing at first, but picking up the pace as we got more comfortable. He responded easily to the messages my knees sent through his ribs. At the middle of the open field he broke into a smooth trot, then into a soft canter. My heart took off on it's own ride. It was my first time on a gaited horse, and it was like rocking in a well oiled swing.

We cantered a couple of times around the field. At the end of the second turn, I threw a glance at the two kids. They were both in the open barn door now, watching every move. A beam of sunlight broke through thin clouds and caught us up in a tunnel of summer brilliance. The girl stood with one small hand raised against the glare that bathed her perfect profile in an aura of gold. My heart soared. I felt a sudden band tighten around my chest, and had to remind my lungs to breathe.

I nudged the powerful body between my knees and bent low over his neck. It was like switching on an afterburner. He shot off across the clearing in a rocketing gallop that sent the dirt flying and my heart racing to keep up.

I clung to his whipping mane as we pounded across the field and skidded to a stop before the open barn doors. I hooked a leg over, slid off his back and hit the ground in one smooth motion, feeling as cool as John Wayne.

The girl's emerald eyes were electric with excitement, one slender finger tracing a circle on her creamy cheek. The boy was studying me again, his head cocked to one side, black eyes glistening.

I tossed them my best smile, took hold of a piece of Diablo's mane and tugged gently. He bobbed his head once, stepped into the barn and turned back into his stall.

"What's your name, wonder boy?" the girl said.

"Royal T. Ripley, believe it or not," I blurted without thinking.

But the name that caused me shudders didn't get even so much as a blink from her.

She swept an arm toward the grimacing boy, "Christian Goodeaux Terwilliger," she said. "Goody. And I'm Cat."

"Actually, it's Carole Ann Terwilliger," he said. "But she thinks it sounds frumpy."

"God, Goody," she said. "Sometimes I could flush you down the toilet."

Then they seemed to forget I was standing right there. Their heads bent together and a small smile hinted around the girl's pink lips.

"I think he's okay," she whispered behind a cupped hand. "Look what he did with the horse."

"One dumb animal to another," he whispered back. "He strikes me as just another Nowhere Mesa redneck showoff."

Dumb animal, redneck showoff? That touched a nerve. I thought it was time to remind them I was listening.

"My Pop says you can tell a lot about a person by how animals respond to them," I said.

They both turned to look at me. The girl's pale eyebrows were raised in surprise.

"Hmm," she said, tracing another circle on her flawless cheek.

"The horse hates us," the boy said. "So that makes us bad according to you?"

"He doesn't hate you," I said. "He knows you're scared to death when you come around him. He doesn't know it's him you're scared of, he just knows you're really scared of something, so he panics, too."

I waited while they digested that one.

"Quick," the girl said, "Name somebody you really admire."

The suddenness and the dare in her question took me by surprise. But the answer was easy, even though she'd probably expect me to say something like Han Solo since Star Wars was still a big thing then. But growing up under Pop's roof taught me that the ones who really matter are the ones with what he called 'the stuff'.

"Anne Frank," I said.

They looked at me like I had just said "Tzswkvbpql."

The girl recovered first. "Why?" she said.

"Because she was just a teen-age kid that had to hide in an attic so the Nazis wouldn't gas her. But instead of giving up, she wrote a great diary that told her story to the whole world."

They were still for awhile then the girl said, "What's the T. in Royal T.?"

"Thomas," I said.

"Thomas," she said, a smile bowing her luscious lips. "I shall call you Tom Ripley."

The boy shook his dark head and sighed. "Okay, Tom Ripley, I guess I'm stuck with you."

We left Diablo with his head hanging out the stall door, watching while we drifted away. We spent the rest of that afternoon trading bits and pieces of our lives. I told them that it was just me and Pop, about us moving here from Missouri, and all about the ranch. They wanted to know about my mother so I told them how she left right after I was born.

Cat did most of the talking for both of them. Once in a while Goody would volunteer some small addition, but she was the one who filled in the blanks.

They were brother and sister, of course, even though you couldn't tell it by looking. I gathered their mother was something of a butterfly, flitting from place to place, and guy to guy. Goody was born in India during their mother's ashram phase. Mother and baby came back to California, but the father didn't. Their mother was actually married to Cat's father but he was killed in Vietnam. They were in "Nowhere Mesa," Arizona for the summer staying with Aunt Jane, while their mother was galavanting around Peru with some new guru she'd found. But Aunt Jane didn't sound very stable, either. She was off visiting her "boyfriend" in Denver for a couple of weeks, leaving them to fend for themselves.

That first afternoon with Cat and Goody was the best time I could remember. In dumb ignorance, I'd thought life was pretty good up to that point. But in the short span of twenty-four hours since I met them, I'd come to realize how empty my life was before. For the first time, I felt I might actually have found some friends as good as the animals I treasured.

It was hard to turn loose when four o'clock rolled around, but I had work to do. So, I tore myself away and peddled my joyful heart home to the ranch.

FOUR

Since I'd met the Terwilliger kids, it was harder every day to keep my mind on the ranch. Each morning seemed longer, but without the tedious morning I couldn't enjoy the free afternoon. So I toiled, and the hours dragged.

But, the morning of the third day of my new life did pass and by one o'clock I was back pounding on the trapdoor in the barn behind the house on Elm Street.

This time I didn't need a made-up excuse to be there. Cat came skinning down the ladder with a welcoming smile, and even Goody seemed to have thawed some. I could tell they were feeling a little awkward though, and I was too. I guess we couldn't quite trust the crack we'd opened in the door that separated us before yesterday. So, we kicked around the barn awhile getting comfortable with each other again.

Cat had her copper hair pulled back in a ponytail, showing a simple gold stud in one dainty earlobe and almost more luscious neck than I could stand.

"Uh, Carole Ann…" I started, but she cut me off.

"See what you did, Goody," she said. "I hate that name; it sounds so geeky. Call me Cat."

I liked Cat a lot better too. "Okay, Cat," I said.

That heady exchange struck me dumb for awhile. Diablo's half open stall door was a welcome diversion. He was still a little shy, too. But an apple slice coaxed him out into the meadow again. Cat and Goody followed and watched while I eased up onto his back and we cantered to the far fence, me hanging on with a handful of black mane and knees pressed against his chest. We trotted back to the barn and pulled up.

"Next," I said.

Goody took a quick step backward, his black eyes tightening. I could feel the muscles in Diablo's chest start to tense. I reached down to pat his neck and the muscles softened.

"Not me," Goody said.

Cat stepped forward, fists clenched at her sides. "I'll go," she said.

My heart kicked up a notch. I reached down for her arm and boosted her up. She settled in behind me with arms at her sides and jeaned legs brushing mine. I nudged Diablo with my knees and he started off in his cushy canter.

I thought the ride was like the back seat of a Coupe de Ville but Cat let out a squeal, threw a death grip around my waist and pressed herself up against my back like her day of reckoning had come. I started to get a lump in my throat and somewhere else all at the same time, and I prayed she couldn't feel my heart pounding or sense the X-rated thoughts scorching through my brain.

Caution got the best of lust. I slowed Diablo to a walk. Cat eased back a little bit but still clung close as we did a slow, sensual rock across the pasture, which suddenly seemed far too small. I offered to let her off when we came back by the barn, but she shook her head and her arms tightened just a little bit around my waist. It took several trips around the pasture before I gave in to my conscience, which was nagging about ignoring Goody.

As we cantered back to the barn, Cat put her lips to my ear. "Goody was kicked in the chest by a horse. For about five minutes they thought he was dead."

"Jeez," I said. "Makes sense that he'd give horses a wide berth."

Back at the barn, I helped Cat down and the warm place she left against my back started to mourn. She pulled Goody aside while I led Diablo back to his stall and slipped him another chunk of apple. A whispered conference was going on when I stepped out of the stall, but it stopped as soon as they saw me.

"In India they don't believe in accidents," Cat said. "They would say you didn't happen into our barn just because of the rain."

No accidents was a brand new thought to me, and it took a minute to digest. But an instant later, I got a flash of what that could mean. I looked at Cat. She was studying me carefully, her lips pressed together, her emerald eyes probing mine while one finger traced another circle on her creamy cheek.

"We thought we might show you the loft," she said. "Want to see it?"

Do the blind want to see? I thought. But I tried to act nonchalant. "Sure," I said.

"Nobody else is allowed," Cat said. She pointed a finger at my nose, a small frown creasing her forehead. "It's a very special place. You have to promise not to say anything to anybody about it."

I don't like promises because they're a very serious matter to me; and sometimes I've found that no matter what, they just won't keep. But they had kicked my curiosity into high gear, so I crossed my fingers and promised.

Cat skipped up the ladder, and stood looking down on us from the lighted opening. "What are you waiting on, Tom Ripley?" she called.

I looked over at Goody and he gave a nod, so up I went with him close on my heels. As I reached the top, Cat stepped back and swept aside a bedsheet curtain, painted with yellow crescent moons and blue stars, that was strung across one large corner of the loft on a long piece of clothesline.

"The Casbah," she said.

Behind the curtain, hay bales were stacked to make a good-sized table that was topped with a black tablecloth that didn't quite cover a sheet of plywood beneath. More bales were arranged around the table to make passable seats. Along two walls back of the table were more hay bales stacked into platforms with sleeping bags unrolled over the tops. An old wooden crate served as an end table between the hay bale beds and on it sat an ugly metal lamp in the shape of a big fish, giving off soft yellow light from under a purple shade with gold tassels hanging down. Books and magazines were scattered around on the beds and seats. A plastic Crosley radio, plugged into a socket on the wall, was playing Elton John's *Yellow Brick Road*.

"Our very own creation," Goody said.

"Neat," I managed.

I said every time I came by they were in the loft, and I wondered what they did up here all the time. The answers were vague, like, "Oh, whatever we want," and "Just stuff." I didn't have time to push the issue because Goody had a doctor's appointment in half an hour and they needed to get going. But they did invite me back the next day. So I floated down from The Casbah with a joyful heart, and started for my bike.

"Tom Ripley," Cat called down from above. They were both leaning over in the yellow square.

She crinkled her fingers down at me. "Tomorrow," she said. And this time my body was on its way back to the ranch, but my heart stayed behind.

FIVE

Another day completely out of hand. I had taken my wife in to town to catch the Phoenix shuttle for a flight to Kansas City to attend her brother's ordination. She was six months pregnant, but it was a major life event she refused to miss.

When I got back to the ranch, I went into the bedroom to get Pop up. He was panting like a winded horse, but I couldn't wake him. I lifted an arm and it fell back on the bed like a soft noodle. There was little doubt but that he'd suffered another stroke.

I couldn't see much point in paying a big fee to the ambulance boys so I called and arranged for his doctor to meet us at the emergency room.

Getting Pop from the bed to the wheelchair, and then to the car was like manhandling a hundred-eighty pound sack of wet feed. But I managed to get him loaded and strapped in. Then we tore out for town.

Verde Mesa's hospital serves a large area of Yavapai County and the emergency unit gets a good workout most days. If you go in with a minor problem you might wait for hours. But they do have their triage priorities in order. Bring them a real emergency and they're right on top of it. Pop was out of the truck, on a gurney, hooked up to IV's, blood pressure, ECG and oxygen monitors

25

within five minutes after we skidded in to the drop off area. His heart was fluttering around like a one-legged chicken so his blood pressure kept spiking and crashing. It was an hour of knots in the stomach before they got him stabilized. Another hour passed before we got him up to intensive care and settled in.

A stroke may be the most cruel affliction there is. Pop's first one came like lightning out of a clear sky. At seventy-three he had slowed down some but still managed on his own. I was just a few weeks out of the hospital myself with a disability discharge from the Army, only about seventy-five percent able, and still pretty lame. We'd been sitting in the living room. Pop decided it was time for bed. He tried to push up off the couch but couldn't make it and sank back into the cushions, gave me a bewildered look and toppled over on his side.

Like Job in the Bible, the thing he most feared in his later years had come to pass. That first stroke took out his left side down to his toes, ravaging his brain so that not much of the old Pop remained. He used to be long on patience but the stroke took that too, so his frustration level was near the explosion point most of the time. With a wrenching effort that had tears running down every cheek in the room, he could form some words but they were slurred and garbled, almost impossible to understand. It was two weeks before he could even stay upright in the bed without pillow supports, or focus on a moving object. Many an hour I sat by his bed wrestling with the thought that not a person I knew would ever consider letting an animal suffer in that condition.

One thing the stroke didn't take was his Missouri stubbornness. So like a snail inching forward, the therapists gradually got him into a wheel chair and able to make intelligible sounds. But he hit a plateau at six weeks and all the encouraging progress came to a screeching halt. They worked him over for another week but in the end we were left with the choice of nursing home or back to the ranch. I loaded all his paraphernalia into the truck and took him home.

It was too early to tell how this second stroke might turn out, but so far it looked pretty bad. He drifted in and out of semi-consciousness, had no reflexes in his arms or legs, and his breathing was still as raggedy as a freight train pulling a long grade.

I dropped into a chair by Pop's bed, closed my aching eyes, and settled in for another long siege, grateful that my wife was missing out on this part of the adventure.

A big part of hospitals is the waiting. My wife and I have done this so many times with Pop that we're old pros at it. But we don't just sit. We spend a lot of time in our own special silence anyway, not just when things seem out of control. We call it meditation; some might call it prayer. Whatever you call it we usually find some comfort there. Sometimes we even find wisdom, but usually it's just a soul-soothing silence. I've come to believe that's how the Universe keeps me enough on track so I don't derail completely.

So, in spite of the life and death struggles going on around me, or maybe because of them, I leaned back and closed my eyes, expecting to slip into my normal meditation mode. But my mind rebelled. It seemed like ever since I bashed my head delivering Kate's calf, my mind slipped back to 1978 whenever I closed my eyes. But I didn't try to fight it. Those memories are the touchstone of my life.

I'd left Cat and Goody the last time with a promise to return the next afternoon, but my plans got changed. I was hoeing the corn next morning when the skies began to roll and crash. Lightning started to spit and crackle and I only just made it back to the house before the torrent unleashed. In sight of three minutes, the ditch that caught the runoff from the slope next to the house was raging like the Mississippi at flood stage. As I watched from the shelter of the porch, the muddy water breached the edge of the ditch, poured down the slope, and cut a deep trench right through the middle of the gravel driveway.

The flood was over in ten minutes but it took me the rest of the day to fix the damaged driveway and shore up the drainage ditch. So, it was the next afternoon when I banged on the trapdoor to the barn loft on Elm Street.

This time the door scraped open to a welcoming "Hey" from both smiling faces. Cat's copper hair was in pigtails wrapped with green bows, and her emerald eyes were shining even in the dim light of the barn. Her slender hands waving me up the ladder sent my heart into overdrive. Gone, like magic, was a gulf that just days ago might have been too wide to ever bridge across. Over the course of four short days, I'd been promoted from suspicious rejection to cautious acceptance, and now to wide-open friendship.

Cat wanted to know where I was the day before, and I told them all about the storm and the damage. I asked what they'd been doing and two sets of eyes turned to their hay bale table. Laid out on the tabletop were some kind of alphabet board game, and a spread out deck of cards that I didn't recognize. The little radio was playing a Kenny Loggins tune that I always liked a lot but couldn't remember the name of.

"What's that stuff?" I asked.

Cat unsnapped a safety pin that held two sections of the bed sheet curtain together. "First things first," she said. "You have to swear an oath."

Promises and oaths sounded like a grade school initiation. I wanted to say so, but her eyes told me she was dead serious so I pulled back.

"To be binding it has to be a blood oath, so give me your hand." She took my finger, squeezed the tip until it turned white, then in one quick move stabbed the finger with the sharp point of the pin. A crimson drop oozed from the tiny wound.

"Now lick off the blood and swear, I Royal Thomas Ripley, promise I will never reveal the existence of The Casbah, or any of its secrets."

I still didn't much like it but I licked the blood off my finger, raised my right hand, swore my solemn oath, and started to drop my hand.

"You're not finished," Cat said. "I also promise to keep an open mind to everything I see and hear take place."

She had my curiosity going full blast now. I repeated the words and dropped my hand.

"Okay, what's the stuff on the table?" I said.

"Ouija board and tarot cards," Cat said.

I didn't know what Ouija boards or tarot cards were. "How do you play?"

"They're not games, silly," Cat said. "They're for....."

They looked at each other for a long minute. Finally Goody said, "Contacting spirits."

I waited to see if they were pulling my leg. But their eyes were stone serious.

"You mean you talk to dead people?" I said.

"Not dead people, live spirits," Goody said. "Spirits from the other side of life."

Hmm, I thought. My face must have given me away because Cat shot me a look, and I understood why she made me swear.

"Really, no lie?" I said.

"No lie," Goody said. "But that's not something we tell every-body, nobody, actually."

He'd be very right about that, I thought.

I'd found that people in Verde Mesa weren't as rigid as where we came from in Missouri, but there still seemed to be little patience with behaviors outside their notion of acceptable boundaries.

"It was that kick from the horse, when they thought he was dead," Cat said. "At first I thought he was crazy too. All he wanted to talk about was his 'incredible experience' and how wonderful it was."

Goody's eyes shone. "I was dead, for certain." he said. "If it happened to you you'd think it was the most incredible experience, too. My mind separated from my body and didn't want to come back."

That idea was no big deal to me. One of Pop's main themes was that everything, including us, is just a different vibration of the same invisible energy that makes up our Universe; some things we can see and some we can't. He says the experience we call death is really just a change in the vibration of our mind to match the vibration of a dimension that's all thought energy instead of the physical energy we're used to here. Pop was usually right about such things.

"So, this is what we do," Cat said. "Try to contact Goody's spirit world."

"Have you done it?" I asked.

They looked at each other; neither seemed to want to answer. Finally Goody shrugged. "We get some messages on the Ouija board but mostly they don't make much sense."

I asked if I could watch while they did it and they said okay, but not to expect too much.

Goody pointed me to a seat at the hay bale table, and sat down across. Cat slid onto a bale between us.

Goody pulled the Ouija board toward him, put his fingers lightly on its plastic pointer, and closed his eyes. "You ask it a question," he said. "Then wait for the pointer to spell out an answer on the board."

Goody sat perfectly still. He thought a minute, then said, "My question is, why isn't this working?"

Cat lifted her eyebrows at me and we both bent to watch Goody's fingers on the pointer. Several minutes crept by. As far as I could tell, nothing was happening. Goody hadn't moved an eyelash and the pointer seemed glued to the board. More minutes passed in silence. Goody sighed, his eyes opened and his fingers slipped off the pointer.

"Have you tried it with two people?" I said.

"You mean four hands on the pointer?" Cat said.

"Why not?" Goody said. "You two do it."

"Okay," Cat said and touched her fingers to the top of the pointer, then looked over at me.

As I placed my eight fingers down on the pointer, two fingertips brushed hers. It felt like touching an electric fence wire. A warm tingle ran up one arm, across my back, and down through my other hand. I looked up at Cat. She was staring like she'd never seen me before. Our eyes held for a moment, and this time a warm tingle ran down my spine. Her shoulders twitched just a little, and I wondered if by some miracle she felt the same tingle I did. Then she dropped her eyes and fixed on the Ouija pointer.

I was still thinking about that warm tingle when it slowly dawned on me that the tingling I'd felt wasn't just a warm memory, my fingers really were tingling. And, the pointer was moving slowly on the board.

I looked up at Cat. Her eyes were glued to the pointer. "You're doing that, aren't you?" she said.

"I thought you were," I said.

"Shh," Goody said. "Close your eyes, try not to think about anything."

I closed my eyes and tried to lose myself, like I could sometimes. But my mind was stuck on what was happening with the pointer. I could feel it moving under my fingertips, ever so slowly across the board, stopping briefly, then moving on again.

After a time, the minutes seemed to stop passing, and I lost track of everything except the pointer inching slowly over the board.

"……..wrote it down, that's what it spelled out," Goody was saying as I drifted back.

"Is it really a message, do you think?" Cat said.

"You didn't do it deliberately?" Goody said.

"No," Cat said. "I felt like I was dreaming."

"Me too," I said. "What did we spell."

Goody turned the sheet of paper so I could see it. *NAMASTE*, it read.

"What do you think it means?" Cat said.

"Gibberish," Goody said.

"It sounds like a real word," Cat said. "Let's try it again."

I was all for charging ahead too, and wanted to see what else the board would say.

Goody put on the brakes. "Not me," he said. "I've had it with this silly stuff."

"But we got a message," Cat said.

"I doubt it," Goody said. "Anyway, nothing could ever match the real thing. It was like the most beautiful dream. I was floating in space, and voices like chocolate crème whispered wonderful secrets, but I couldn't quite understand. Somehow I have to…."

"Just stop it," Cat said, stabbing his chest with a finger. "You promised."

Promised what, I thought. But I didn't ask.

Goody's black eyes flashed. "Screw this," he said.

He turned away and headed down the ladder. It seemed like a good time for me to exit, too. I started to follow.

Cat touched my arm. "Please come back tomorrow," she said.

"Wild horses couldn't keep me away," I said. That brought a small smile.

As I was going down the ladder she leaned into the opening above my head and made a zipping motion over her mouth. God, she was cute.

"Keep a zipped lip," she said. "What ever happens in The Casbah stays in The Casbah."

I wasn't about to tell anybody what happened that afternoon. But I zippered my lips back at her and headed for the ranch.

SIX

I was startled from my reverie by the piercing beep of a monitor above Pop's head. A nurse was standing by the bed, pushing the call button. Pop's face was a gray mask in the gloom blanketing the bed, his lips blue. Weak afternoon light, slanting through pulled blinds, tried but couldn't quite cut the shadows that filled the room.

Suddenly, nurses were buzzing around all over the place, turning up glaring lights and easing me back out of the way. A doctor came and shooed me out of the room.

I went without argument. The outcome of this adventure was not in my hands. With the baby due in a few months, we were hoping the promise that new life brings into a house might get Pop back on the road to recovery again. But The Grand Planner didn't seem to be paying any attention to our agenda. It felt like I was caught in a runaway express with no engineer at the throttle. I've found there's only one thing to do in times like these, let go of my resistance and try to put my mind out of gear.

But lately my mind seemed to have only the one gear. And just like it had been doing more and more often, that gear meshed again. This time to the afternoon following the adventure with the Ouija board.

I found Cat and Goody in The Casbah once again. That day the radio was silent and they were still at odds. Cat wanted to have another go at the Ouija board, but Goody was trying to duck out, saying there was something he needed to do. They went back and forth awhile, then I suggested we go to the library to see if we could find out what "Namaste" meant. Cat jumped at the chance, Goody grudgingly agreed, and we set out for downtown.

"Namaste sounds like mixed up pig latin to me," Goody said, "Ancay, ooyay, alktay, igpay, atinlay."

"It's not pig latin," Cat said. "Maybe it's some ancient foreign language like the Dead Sea Scrolls they found. Aramaic, or something."

"Not much chance to find out what it means in the Nowhere Mesa library." Goody said.

"You might be surprised at the 'Nowhere Mesa' library," I said. "It just so happens that my Pop is the librarian. Among other things, he's a walking encyclopedia. If he doesn't know the answer, he'll know where to find it."

Cat looked at me like I might have just said I was really a bewitched prince. "Aren't you just full of surprises," she said.

"Hmph," Goody said.

"I knew you didn't find your way into our barn by accident," Cat said.

"I hope that's true," I said.

"That's what she thinks," Goody said. "That there is one great big plan, and we're all just little pieces of it waiting to fit together. That's not how it seemed when I died. For a little while it was all so clear and simple how everything worked. It was like when you suddenly understand something the teacher said that never made sense before. You know, when you go 'Aha, now I get it'."

Cat turned on him, eyes flashing. "You just won't quit, will you. Even if......." Her voice trailed off

If what, I thought. *What's this all about?*

We were just passing the Rexall Drugstore, and it seemed like a good place for a time-out.

"How about a soda-pop?" I said. "My treat."

We sat at a little table by the soda fountain and quietly nursed our drinks, no one feeling like talking for awhile. Cat had a cherry coke, Goody had a limeade, and I had an ice-cold root beer.

Finally I said, "Cat's right, Goody. You need to stop talking about when you died. People don't understand, and it's scary. Plus it makes you seem weird."

Cat cocked her head at me. "If you only knew how weird," she said.

"How can I ever hope to be normal, again?" Goody said in a near whisper.

Cat opened her mouth, but Goody held up a hand. "Okay, okay, back to the Ouija board," he mumbled.

"Truce," I said.

Cat shook her head. "Has it ever occurred to you that it may not work because your mind is closed to the possibility?" she said to Goody. "You could at least give it a fair chance."

I thought, *Pop says an open mind offers richer rewards than the Comstock Lode.* But I didn't say it.

Instead, I said, "I have my doubts, too. But you have to be curious about where 'Namaste' came from, just like I am."

Goody smiled sheepishly. "Well, yeah, I guess I am, a little," he said.

Cat poked me in the ribs. "Are you sure you didn't do that on purpose with the Ouija pointer?"

"Cross my heart and hope to die, stick a needle in my eye," I said.

Cat grinned. "Stuuupiiid," she said.

But they were okay now and we headed on down to the library.

Pop had done a lot with the town library in the past couple of months. There was a separate reference section now; an alcove especially for teenagers, and a closet-sized children's corner with tables and chairs to fit the small fry.

Pop was hunched over his desk in the small office behind the checkout counter when we came in. He looked up when he heard the door close, and his face crinkled into the smile that made you feel like you just made his day.

"Pop," I said. "This is Carole Ann and Goody."

Cat locked her hands behind her back and said, "Cat. Hi."

"Hi, back," Pop said.

Goody stuck out his hand. "Christian Goodeaux Terwilliger," he said.

Pop took Goody's hand in both of his. And something happened. A millisecond ripple seemed to travel down the muscles of Goody's arm and up Pop's. I could have imagined it except for a sudden tic in Pop's eyelid that I recognized as surprise.

Pop formed a tent with his hands, inclined his head and said, "Namaste".

My knees went weak. Pop surprised me a lot, but this was a shock like no other. I couldn't find my voice.

Goody's chin dropped half way to his chest. Cat's mouth froze in a perfect *O*.

I found my voice, but it sounded strange. "You're not gonna believe this, Pop," I said. "But we heard that word for the first time yesterday and we came here hoping to find out what it meant."

Pop smiled. "It's Sanskrit," he said. "An ancient Buddhist salutation but still common today in India. It means *I honor the divinity in you*."

"But that's so weird," Cat said. "You used the very same word we came here to find out about."

Pop shrugged as if there were no great mystery. "Goody gave it to me when I took his hand. Where did you come across it?" he said.

The other two looked at me to volunteer. I was always safe with Pop so I took up the challenge.

"I'm sure you know about Ouija boards," I said.

Pop nodded.

"We were experimenting with the Ouija board yesterday and the pointer spelled out Namaste."

"Hmm," Pop said.

"Tom and I were using the pointer and that's what it spelled," Cat said.

"Tom?" Pop said. He liked Royal about as much as I hated it.

I know I flushed, I could feel my ears burning. But no one else seemed to notice.

Goody looked at Pop like a puppy wanting to please his master. "My sister thinks she has to distract me with voodoo games," he said. "I was kicked by a horse last year. My heart actually stopped, and now I know what comes after. It was…I felt like……..I've never felt so……..alive."

"Oh, Goody," Cat whispered. A tear started down her cheek and she turned her head away.

Pop put a hand on her shoulder. "No, it's okay. I understand," he said.

That was Pop. Understanding, wise, and oh so gentle with the most private information. I wanted to hear more, but the door swung open and two crew cut boys bounced in.

"Why don't you bring your friends around on Sunday," Pop said. "We can have a nice chat."

SEVEN

"As if another stroke wasn't enough, it looks like your dad also suffered a heart attack," the young doctor was saying. "It's a fairly common sequela to ischemic stroke. When a shower of blood clots starts, it's almost a given that some will find their way to the small arteries that feed the heart itself. If a clot is large enough to block one of those little arteries, a section of the heart will go into spasms and the heart can't pump efficiently. When the heart can't pump enough oxygenated blood to the rest of the body, especially to a brain that's already suffered a stroke, you have a life-threatening situation. We got him stabilized again but there's no way to predict an outcome."

"We're expecting a new baby soon," I said. "We were so hoping he could be here to see it."

"It's not impossible," the doctor said. "With the anti-clotting treatment he's on he could survive this crisis. Of course, we can't tell what damage he's suffered yet, either to his brain or his heart. We'll need more time to determine that."

I took his hand in both of mine. "Thanks for caring about him," I said.

"It's what I do," he said, and turned away down the hallway.

I returned to Pop's bedside where the life-sustaining machines continued to pump and sigh. The sounds were hypnotic, and pretty soon my eyes wouldn't stay open. It was no surprise anymore that every time I closed my eyes my mind made a beeline backward, once again.

After our meeting with Pop at the library, I was in a sweat to get back to the loft and have another go at the Ouija board. Goody was in a daze and followed along like a sleepwalker, but Cat was full of questions, chattering like her spring was wound too tight.

"You're so lucky to have a dad like that," she said. "He made me feel like he really cared about us. And that he understands. And really wants to help us. And, I feel like maybe there's hope after all."

"He used to be a priest," I said.

"A Catholic Priest?" she said.

"Episcopal," I said. "Thirty-six years worth."

"We don't go to church," she said.

"We don't either, since we left Missouri," I said. "Pop says as soon as he started meditating he began to outgrow organized religion. He says it stops short of the real truth."

"What's meditating?" Cat said.

"Well," I said. "It's sort of like erasing your mind, then waiting to see what gets written on it."

"Sounds like Ouija without the board," Cat said.

That surprised me. "I guess so," I said. "Pop says meditation is shutting down the human mind so we can connect with the One True Mind. He could probably meditate for hours. He says the One True Mind has all the answers if we can only turn off our own chatter long enough to listen. It's our human mind that leads us astray."

Goody spoke for the first time since we left the library. "Is that what he wants to talk to us about?" he said.

"Maybe, and probably other stuff, too," I said.

"But what about the 'Namaste' business?" Cat said. "How could he know about that?"

"Something happened when he took my hand," Goody said. "It was like a current ran up and down my arm."

"I know, I saw it," I said.

"Do you really think some people are psychic?" Cat said.

"Well, it's always seemed like Pop knows stuff other people don't," I said. "He can put his hand on my shoulder and know what I'm thinking. He knows who's on the telephone or at the door before it's answered. Sometimes he knows other stuff before it happens. So, yeah, I suppose you could call him psychic. I never thought much about it, it was just Pop being Pop."

Goody grabbed Cat's arm. "And he said he believed me about the accident," he said.

"Oh, Goody, don't you know I want to believe it, too?" Cat said. "But it still seems like a sick hallucination, it's made you so crazy."

Goody shook his head. "I didn't imagine I was dead. Remember my heart stopped. It was too real to be a hallucination. And I know what I felt was wonderful, I just can't quite remember how it was."

"I bet Pop can help," I said. "There's one thing you can stake your life on: if he says something is so, you can take it to the bank."

"Not 'til Sunday," Cat said. "But now, how about another try with the Ouija board?"

"I'm in," I said.

"Don't you guys every give up?" Goody said. "You know it's probably just some kind of mental telepathy. Psychics do it all the time, why couldn't we?"

"Spell out a word we've never even heard?" Cat said.

"Why not," he said. "Tom probably knew the word and just didn't tell us."

"But Tom didn't know it," I said. "And even if I did, that still doesn't explain how two people could guide the pointer to the right letters with their eyes closed. I think we're on to something here."

He might not be convinced but I was mightily impressed by the 'Namaste' business.

"Always the doubter," Cat said to Goody. "I'll make you a deal. Let's ask it one more question and if we don't get an answer I'll stop pushing the Ouija board. Okay?"

"You're taking a big risk," Goody said. "If it doesn't give us the right answer will you guys give up on this silly game once and for all?"

"Shake," I said, and we all did.

"Deal," Cat said.

I said a quick prayer that the board wouldn't fail us. And we were soon back in the loft with eight fingers resting on the big plastic pointer while Goody directed the process.

Goody began writing on a piece of paper. "This time you won't know what the question is," he said.

Cat and I bent over the board and closed our eyes. Once more the pointer began to move slowly across the board. I risked a peek at Cat. Her eyes were closed, her body relaxed.

I lost track of time again, as the pointer continued to move in lazy circles over the board. My arms seemed detached, doing their own thing with the pointer while the rest of me floated, having no purpose except to breathe in and out.

The next thing I knew Cat was speaking. "I know we spelled something, I felt the pointer move."

Goody held up a piece of paper. "You spelled, *JN161213.* Not much of a mystery. It's gibberish again."

Cat wasn't ready to give up. "But it did spell something," she said.

"What was the question?" I said.

Goody handed me the paper he had written on. "Is there really another place where we go when we die?" I read.

"Still, I think it must mean something," I said. "It's another question for Pop, on Sunday."

"Can your dad interpret dreams?" Goody said.

"Sometimes," I said. Sometimes dreams made sense to me, too. But I didn't say it.

"I've been having these dreams," Goody said, "Ever since my accident. They're always different but they have the same theme. There's a message for me, but something always keeps me from it. Last night I was in a long, dark tunnel. There was a neon sign at the far end of the tunnel that I was desperately trying to reach. I knew I had to read it or die. I struggled and struggled but the sign got farther and farther away. It was like trying to run underwater. Suddenly, I broke free and raced toward the sign. I was half way there when the sign exploded out toward me and filled the whole end of the tunnel. I could read it clearly. It said: *When The Student is Ready, The Teacher Will Appear.* Does it make any sense to you?"

I thought it was pretty obvious. "Well," I said, "You know you've been searching for answers ever since your accident. Maybe the dreams are telling you that the time wasn't right 'til now. Ask Pop about it on Sunday."

"Sunday at Ripley's believe it or not," Goody said. "I hope it's something I can believe."

EIGHT

I had to leave Pop's hospital room for a couple of hours in the cool gray dawn to go back and take care of the animals. So I missed the young doctor on his morning rounds. But I didn't need him to tell me that Pop wasn't getting any better. He did seem peaceful, though, as the machines hummed and sighed around him. Once again I wondered about the wisdom of keeping inert flesh going when the spirit is pulling away.

After the nurses were finished fussing around, I tried reading the paper. But I couldn't concentrate on trivia. I settled back into the recliner, hoping for a nap, but it wouldn't come. My mind was still on its one-track trip with shorter breaks between. So there I was again, reliving those few weeks of the summer that defined my life from then forward.

Saturday dragged as I plodded through my household chores and spent the rest of the morning picking, shucking, and bagging two bushels of golden sweet corn to put in the freezer. At seventeen, working in the garden was not pleasure, and I had to keep reminding myself how good the corn would taste in the middle of winter.

By one o'clock Saturday afternoon I was banging on the barn loft trapdoor, hoping to interest Cat and Goody in the matinee at the

Plaza Theater. But the loft was empty. So I backtracked to the house and knocked on the rear door.

Cat came to the door in cut off jeans and an oversized, UC Berkeley T-shirt. Her copper curls were tied up in a ponytail that caressed the back of her neck whenever she turned her head.

"Hi," she said through the screen door.

"Hi," I said. "I thought you guys might like to take in the Saturday matinee."

"Goody's at the library," she said. "What's on?"

"Superman," I said.

"Oh, sure," she said. "Well, I'll go if you want."

Do the starving crave food? I thought. "Okay," I said.

The balcony was bustling with noisy kids. I could feel the stares and whispers follow us to the last row where the older, bolder kids went to neck. I'd been here once before and sat quietly up front, ignoring the bedlam around me. Not this time, though. With Cat by my side I wasn't Clark Kent anymore; I was Superman. Even if I was a little weak in the knees.

Remember the interminable wait when it seemed like the show would never start? It was twice as long that Saturday before the lights went down.

Even with Christopher Reeve flying through the air for a couple of hours, I couldn't remember much about the movie afterwards because I was so excited I couldn't concentrate very well. It took about an hour before I worked up the nerve to drape my arm across the back of Cat's seat. And another half hour or so before I could risk sliding my hand onto her shoulder. She'd seemed completely engrossed in the movie 'til she felt my hand. Then she sat forward and looked at me for a long moment, but without any expression to let me know if I had struck out or not. Finally, she reached up and twined her fingers around mine, settled into her seat and turned back to the movie. My heart did a drum roll, and the fantasies flew like the actor on the screen. My pulse was just beginning to throttle down when the movie ended, and the house lights jarred me back to reality.

We held hands all the way back to Cat's house. I was feeling like I'd just run a mile at top speed, but she seemed calm as evening, chattering about the movie.

"It looked like he was really flying. I wonder how they do that. Wouldn't that be great?" she said. "To be able to fly."

"Yeah," I said. "Must be some feeling."

"Goody thinks he knows," she said.

I didn't understand, and must have shown it.

"The accident," she said. "He says he felt like he was flying."

Goody's accident again. I really didn't want to hear any more about it. I wanted to talk about us.

Goody wasn't back when we got to the house. So I sat on the porch steps while Cat went inside for a minute. She came out with two cokes and sat down beside me. The afternoon sun filtered through the big cottonwoods lining the lane to the barn. A hummingbird flitted around a red-liquid feeder hanging from a corner of the porch.

"Goody tried to kill himself six months ago," Cat said. "Everybody else thought it was an accident, but it wasn't."

I was stunned to silence.

"I knew he was doing drugs for some time, but he was seeing a psychiatrist, and I hoped it would pass."

I found my voice. "What did he do?" I said.

Cat ran a slow hand through her copper hair. "OD'd on mom's sleeping pills," she said.

"Jeez," I said. I'd never known anyone who did drugs before.

"Oh yeah," she said. "He was a straight arrow up until his accident. After he got out of the hospital it was like he went looney all of a sudden. He had this sick fixation on death, and started raiding mom's purse for drug money. At first it was just pot. But it didn't take him long to graduate to the harder stuff."

This was new territory to me. "Like what?" I said.

"Uppers, downers, coke, acid," she said. "I think he must have been dealing, too, because pocket change couldn't have kept him stoned half the time like he was."

"And your mom didn't know?" I said.

Cat dismissed that with a wave of her hand. "Oh, she knew he was messed up after the accident. But, she passed the problem off to a psychiatrist and went back to work. She was gone most of the time, anyway, working or in some meeting or other. We were on our own mostly, just like we are now."

I was still stunned. I'd heard about things like this, but they didn't happen to anyone I knew.

"It was the acid that made him really crazy," she said. "He said it was almost like dying again. That's when he got into the sleeping pills. It's just lucky I got home early and found him."

"You think he did it on purpose?" I said.

"I'm sure he did," she said. "All he thinks about is finding that feeling he had when he died."

"And no one else caught on?" I said.

"Goody told mom he was having nightmares all the time, which he actually was," she said. "And he took the pills hoping they would help. Even the psychiatrist bought it."

"What happened then," I said.

"He was in the hospital for two weeks that time," she said. "Long enough to dry out, I guess. After he came home, he actually did seem better. Everybody decided it was a great idea to send us off to Aunt Jane's for the rest of the summer. Change of scene, healthy environment and all that. And, a chance for mom to do her thing."

"And…" I said, prompting her to continue.

"And," she said. "Things have been going pretty well, but Goody still has all these morbid fantasies. I thought maybe if I played along it might help. So we set up The Casbah and started trying to contact his spirit world. But when nothing earthshaking happened right away, he started to lose interest. That's about the time you came along."

I wanted to comfort her so bad but I didn't know what to say, so I reached over and took her hand.

She tried to smile. "I'm afraid something bad is going to happen," she said.

"Pop and me, we'll look out for you," I said. Even then, it sounded dumb.

She smiled and patted my hand.

I stood up. "I gotta be going," I said. "Pop said I could drive the pickup over and get you tomorrow. About one?"

She stood beside me. "Sure, I'll tell Goody," she said.

Impulse grabbed me. I leaned down and kissed her. Her soft lips parted in surprise for an instant, then melted into mine. The world stopped for a moment while two young hearts merged. After a time she tilted her head back to look into my eyes. Tiny freckles dotted her upturned nose.

"I didn't think I liked you at first, Royal T.," she said.

"I sometimes get off to a slow start, but I tend to grow on people," I said.

She laughed. "You've certainly grown on me. Thanks for being such a good friend."

My soul rejoiced. "Forever," I said.

"Hmm," she said.

Superman had nothing on me that day. I rode a cloud of awe and wonder, all the way back to the ranch.

NINE

I was settling into a routine of splitting my time between Pop's hospital room and trying to keep up with the ranch. That usually meant two or three hours in the morning at the ranch, and long days at the hospital. Then a couple of hours at the ranch in the late afternoon, followed by a fitful night on a cot in Pop's room, trying to block out the sighing machines, blinking lights, and nurse's demanding visits. About all I could count on was a few hours of dozing, reliving more tender memories.

Sunday afternoon, Cat, Goody, and I were sitting on our brown, slipcovered sofa eating popcorn, with Pop across from us in his recliner, the reading lamp hanging above his shoulder.

I had just asked Pop if he could explain the "Namaste" message from the Ouija board.

"Well," Pop said. "I guess what you're really asking me is if I think you got a message from another realm. And, you obviously did get a message. 'Namaste'. As to where it came from, I don't have a concrete answer for that one. I'm not saying it isn't a message from another dimension. I believe anything is possible. But, it could also be coming from your own unconscious thoughts expressed through the physical medium of a pointer and symbols on a board."

"You mean we all had the same thought at the same time but didn't know it?" Cat said.

Pop smiled at her. "Exactly," he said. "Mental telepathy. And the thought expressed itself by guiding your fingers on the pointer to spell out the word."

"But we didn't even know what it meant," Cat said.

"Sure, you did. You just didn't remember that you knew," Pop said.

"But why would we come up with a word like Namaste?" I said.

"Why not?" Pop said. "What could be more appropriate to three souls fumbling for connection than an ancient salutation, 'I recognize and honor your divinity'?"

We chewed on that one instead of popcorn for awhile.

Then Cat snapped her fingers. "A sign that our souls were relating, even though we didn't know it?" she said.

Once again she took my breath away.

Pop beamed a smile at her. "A+," he said. "A direct message from and to your collective souls. A little sobering, isn't it."

They sat awhile in stunned silence. I could see they were wrestling with the mind-boggling thoughts that, first they actually had an honest to God soul; and second that our souls could communicate, not only with us but also with each other, whether we were aware of it or not.

"And, we got another Ouija message later," I said, showing him the paper Goody had written on. *JN161213.*

Pop studied the paper for a moment. "Or it could be that you've connected with something else completely," he said, almost to himself. "Something I like to call Universal Mind."

He got up and went to his bookcase, then came back with his bible and began flipping pages.

"Here it is," he said. "John 16, verses 12 and 13. Jesus is speaking: *There is so much I want to tell you but you can't understand it now. When the Spirit comes, it shall guide you into all truth.*

Pop put the bible down. We were all quiet for awhile.

"Goody also had a dream that said, 'When the student is ready, the teacher will appear,'" I said.

"Hmm," Pop said. "I've never had much experience with crystal balls and Ouija boards. But I do get messages myself from time to time, sometimes from dreams, sometimes in other ways. Usually when there's some major problem I can't see a solution to."

"I told them about meditation," I said.

Pop smiled at me. "That's usually how I do my connecting with Universal Mind," he said to Cat and Goody. "I believe that's where all knowledge comes from. Maybe the same process is working for you through your Ouija board. Nothing is impossible if you believe in it strongly enough."

We all digested that one for a long moment.

"I understand Christian had a life-altering experience," Pop said. "And he's struggling to comprehend the meaning. If the Ouija board can help, why not?

"But, you don't need a Ouija board to soul talk," Pop continued. "Or to connect with Universal Mind. This may be hard for you to accept, but your searching tells me that you're ready to hear it, so listen close. Our human minds tell us we're independent beings. But we're not that at all. We've somehow forgotten that we are a direct expression of the One invisible Universal Mind. It is us, we are it. It's impossible to exist otherwise. Our one-dimensional ignorance tells us our physical perceptions are the true reality of existence, when the exact opposite is true."

This was familiar ground for me. I'd heard Pop expound on perception versus truth enough to recognize the theme. Goody and Cat sat like Egyptian sphinxes.

"Physical perceptions are the fantasy," Pop said, "Though they seem oh so real to our human brain. The unseen universe of pure thought energy, which is Universal Mind, is the true reality. That's where we come from and that's where we return, though we often reject that possibility because we can't perceive it with our limited human senses. An experience of death like Christian had can give us a glimpse of the spiritual beings we truly are, visible expressions of pure thought and infinite wisdom existing from and in the one Universal Mind. Christian is still in the process of trying to assimilate his experience. It must be an incredibly difficult test."

I watched Goody and Cat to see how they were taking Pop's sermon. They sat ramrod straight, popcorn forgotten, glued to the worn sofa, eyes fixed on Pop.

Pop was on a roll. "Our conscious minds automatically reject the concept of ourselves as thought without physical attachment," he said. "Call it your soul if you like, or your spirit if that's more comfortable. Whatever you choose to call it, it is your true self. Search until you find it. Just never doubt that it exists, in infinite and eternal oneness with Universal Mind, The All That Is And Ever Was, And Ever Shall Be."

Pop paused a moment to study the effect of his sermon on the youthful audience, then decided to continue.

"It's so important that we try to believe in our true nature, even though we may not yet be capable of understanding what that means. I believe that if we persist, we will come to understand, and that knowing will bring a rapture we can't even begin to imagine."

The sermon was over, but nobody moved. Cat and Goody still sat in stiff attention, eyes fixed on Pop. I waited for Pop's next move.

"Intermission," Pop said. "Cake and ice cream, Royal."

I headed for the kitchen. Cat and Goody came back to life. Pop and Goody stayed where they were. Cat came into the kitchen to help me. I could hear Pop and Goody talking in low voices while we dished up the goodies.

"Lemon cake and chocolate ice cream," I said, handing Pop a dish while Cat passed Goody his. With everyone else set, I parked on the sofa next to Cat. We savored the treat for awhile.

Pop finished first, set his dish aside, and watched Goody chasing the last drop of chocolate around the plate.

"Let's talk about your accident," Pop said. "You're not the first one to have a death experience, you know. There are actually quite a few recorded in the literature. Most of them say something about a tunnel, and heading toward a brilliant light, and a feeling of love and oneness with everything."

Goody shot an anxious look at Cat and me. "I don't think I can....."

Pop held up a solemn hand. "We all need to agree on one thing from the start. This is a safe place for each of us. We're here in sacred friendship and love, to help each other. You're free to say or do anything that comes up, without fear of ridicule or judgement. Ever." He locked on each pair of eyes in turn to make sure we understood. "Agreed?"

Three heads dipped in agreement. Pop nodded at Goody. "I'm very interested in your experience," he said.

Goody licked his lips. "Well," he said, "I was in the wrong place, not paying attention, and I got kicked right in the chest by this horse. Everything stopped, like a sudden blackout on the darkest night in history. Then I felt like I was floating, but there didn't seem to be anything supporting me. I could still feel myself, but my mind was in neutral, no thoughts at all. Then, there was this unbelievable light that swallowed me up, and I was part of it. I know it was the most wonderful, perfect feeling there could ever be, but I just can't seem to get it back."

Pop picked up a book laying beside him. "Let me read you something," he said.

Slowly, the black nothingness began to soften, like the last few moments before dawn. Then suddenly, I was in the midst of a light so brilliant white it absorbed everything else in its path, including me. I melted into it with an indescribable joy and peace. I can't guess how long I reveled in my oneness with the infinite light before thoughts began to intrude. With the thoughts came a feeling of growing disappointment, like the slow awakening from a delicious dream. I resisted at first, but questions intruded. Who, what, where, how? The questions flew like frantic moths against a lighted screen.

The silence was as total as the light. But, slowly answers began to seep into my gray awareness, like the warmth that spreads outward from a newly lit fire. And, all of a sudden, I knew. I had returned to the Realm of Pure Thought, the True Reality. I had become the essence of thought and love, merged with all that ever was or ever would be. I was reunited with the One Perfect Source of all that is. Incredible joy filled every pore of my being.

Then, my awareness began to spread outward from the infinite light. I realized that I was not just immersed in The Source. I also still existed as a physical form on a bed in a cold, dark place I knew as Benetton Abbey. No sooner had that awareness dawned than I was ripped from my rapture, and awakened to violent pain that racked my frame.

That brief, glimpse of attainable perfection followed so abruptly by the agonizing return to my pitiful human state, left me with a despondency that nearly drove me to self-destruction.

If only it was possible for words to describe, maybe I could reclaim the ecstasy of those brief moments. But, even though I know I experienced a sensation so miraculous and perfect, I'm unable to recapture the feeling. The rational part of my brain knows that its human limitations allow no possibility of repeating the experience. Yet, I was compelled to continue the search. Unbearable frustration lay in the certainty of never being able to experience that sensation in the human form. So, the time finally came when I had to let it go and accept that death was the only ticket to the rapture I yearned for, and death kept its own schedule.

Goody was nodding his head like an eager pupil. "Yes, yes," he said. "That's how it was. I can almost get it, but it's always just out of reach."

Cat had slid forward to the very edge of the couch. "Who wrote that?" she said.

"A French Monk by the name of Frobert," Pop said. "In the thirteenth century."

I drove a couple of very subdued spiritual novices back to town. Neither spoke until we stopped at their door.

Goody opened the pickup door then turned to me and shook his head. "I don't think I'll ever get it right," he said.

"I know," I said. "I've been hearing it for seventeen years and it's still hard for me to see myself as a spiritual being looking for human experience, rather than a human being looking for spiritual experience."

"But that's the only thing that makes any sense," Cat said. "Otherwise we're just animals acting on instinct."

Another surprise from Carole Ann Terwilliger. My heart leaped at her words. It seemed Pop had a willing convert.

"Oh, how I yearn to know the truth," Goody said. "But I still think there's only one way to find out for sure."

"I know what you're thinking," I said. "And you're wrong. That's not the answer anymore than mind-warping chemicals are. Pop can help you, it just takes time for it to come together."

"I don't think anything will work for me," Goody said.

"Dammit, Goody," Cat said. "It's time you stopped feeling sorry for yourself. You've just heard a very wise man offer you a mountain of hope, and all you can do is wallow in the same old miserable crap."

Goody just shook his head, slumped out of the truck and started for the house.

"Pop wants you back next Sunday," I hollered after him, but he kept on going.

"I hope we'll see you before then," Cat said.

"How about tomorrow?" I said.

She leaned over and kissed me gently.

Goody might be miserable, but boy was I ever feeling good.

TEN

I didn't realize I had been asleep 'til I woke to a nurse bending over, checking Pop's vital signs. Outside the window it was the darkest part of the night, the time when your spirit is weakest.

The nurse bustled out, letting the door slam behind her. I was awake for good now, but with my eyes closed my mind rewound once more, and the memory reel picked up where it had left off twelve years ago.

The Monday after Pop's Sunday sermon at the ranch, Bruiser, the friendly old mouser we inherited dragged into the barn all beat up again from a night of tomcatting. Pop decided Bruiser'd had enough of life in the fast lane and asked me to take him in to the vet to get him patched up and fixed. I called and made an appointment.

So, early that afternoon I boxed Bruiser up and was soon banging on The Casbah door with an invitation for Cat and Goody to attend Bruiser's alteration. Cat politely declined. But Goody jumped at the chance, seemingly recovered from his bout of Sunday's doldrums.

I left my bike in the barn and we walked downtown, Bruiser crying his laments through the holes in the box. Doc Johnson has a new clinic on the west side of town now, but back then his office was a small walkout beneath Haley's Hardware store.

"This won't take long," Doc said. "He'll be pretty dopey after but you can take him home. Want to wait out here, or come and watch?" Then he chuckled, "Long as you promise not to faint."

Like he'd expected, we promised and followed him through a door that led to a room full of stainless steel and glass cabinets, shelves lined with instruments and bottles.

Doc opened a cabinet and pulled out a syringe and a bottle of clear liquid with a green label. "Ketamine," he said. "Neat stuff. Dopers love it. It's almost identical to a street drug they call PCP, or Angel Dust. I like it because it works fast, it's completely safe and the effects wear off in a couple of hours."

He loaded the syringe about half full then laid out a surgical knife and a small forceps. He had me open Bruiser's box and set him on the steel table. Then he got a handful of skin on Bruiser's neck, lifted him into the air, popped him in the hind leg with the shot, dropped him back in the box and closed the top, all before the cat had a chance to know what was happening. Five minutes later Bruiser was limp as a cooked noodle and feeling no pain.

"Hold his tail out of the way," Doc said.

"Count me out," Goody said. He backed away from the table and busied himself checking out the stuff in the cabinets. I grabbed Bruiser's tail and pulled it to one side.

With the tail out of the way, Doc squeezed Bruiser's little scrotum into a knot and plucked a bald spot over one ball. Then he picked up the knife, made a quick bloodless cut through the skin, popped the marble out of its sack, clamped it off with the forceps, cut it free and tossed it into a bucket under the table. Then did the same thing again to the other one.

That part was over almost before it started. But while Bruiser was still sawing logs, Doc cleaned up the worst of the fight wounds and gave him a shot of penicillin.

We put Bruiser back in the box and were on our way not more than twenty minutes from the time we walked in the door. That ketamine is pretty slick stuff.

Goody was in a jaunty mood on the way back. I hadn't seen that side of him before, cracking wise in a falsetto voice about changing Bruiser's name to Bruce and getting a pink collar for his neck.

With Bruiser due to wake up hopping mad, I didn't have time to visit with Cat and Goody in The Casbah. I strapped the box on the back of my bike and headed for the ranch.

That night at dinner I told Pop all about the adventure at the vet's, and how Doc Johnson said Bruiser should become the perfect gentleman in a few days.

"Your young friend was in the library again this afternoon," Pop said. "He's been in several times lately reading this and that. This time he was asking about ketamine. The visit to the vet must have piqued his curiosity."

A warning bell jingled in a dark corner of my mind. "That's what Doc used to knock Bruiser out," I said.

"Angel dust it's called on the street," Pop said. "It's popular with the counter culture crowd. We found it in the *Physician's Desk Reference*. And a lot of information about the psychotic effects in a *Psychology Today* article. People who've taken it are likely to hallucinate a separation of mind and body, and have visions like near-death experiences."

"Uh, Pop," I said. "There's something you should know about Goody."

Pop looked up from his plate, his eyebrows raised.

"Cat says he tried to kill himself a few months back. Apparently he got into heavy drugs trying to repeat the experience when his heart stopped and he thought he was with God. She thinks he deliberately OD'd on their mom's sleeping pills. She's afraid he's so mixed up he might try again."

"Christian?" Pop said. "Surely not. He may be having trouble comprehending his near death experience, but I can't believe he's suicidal."

As wise as he is, sometimes Pop's stubborn belief in the goodness of human nature leaves him blind as a mole.

"Maybe, but he sure is interested in ketamine," I said. "And it sounds like exactly what he's been looking for."

"Well," Pop said. "It's not something you can just go buy at the drugstore. It's not likely he could get his hands on it even if he tried."

I knew Pop was probably right, but I went to bed that night with a hollow feeling at the pit of my stomach.

ELEVEN

The longer the night by Pop's bedside dragged on, the more trouble I was having keeping the present separated from the past. Finally, I just gave in and let the past take over.

The morning after the visit to Doc Johnson's, I woke with a jolt, remembering how happy Goody was after we left Doc's office the day before, and a chill ran down my spine. I had an idea where Goody could get some Angel Dust, and I suspected he was way ahead of me. I jumped up and ran to the phone.

Cat answered on the sixth ring.

"What's Goody up to?" I said without introduction.

"And good morning to you, too," she said. "I guess he's still in bed, like I was 'til the phone rang."

"Sorry," I said. "I woke up with a bad feeling this morning. It wouldn't wait."

"Okay," she said. "You're forgiven. Are you coming over later?"

"Sure," I said. "How did Goody seem last night?"

"He was upstairs in his room reading," she said. "Happy as a clam."

"That's what worries me," I said, and told her about Doc Johnson's ketamine and Pop's report of Goody's research at the library.

"Uh oh," Cat said. She was quiet for a moment. Then she said, "That stuff sounds like his dream come true."

"Doc Johnson had a shelf full of it," I said. "In an open cabinet right next to us. And the needles to use it."

"I'll go check on him," she said. "I'll call you right back."

The phone clicked off and I waited. Pop trekked by on his way to the bathroom and asked what was going on. I told him I was waiting for a call from Cat. Ten minutes passed before the phone rang.

Cat sounded like she'd just run a mile at top speed. "He's not here," she said. "I checked everywhere, even The Casbah. His bed hasn't been slept in, either."

"I'll be there quick as I can," I said, and clicked off.

I told Pop what was going on and what I suspected. He asked me to call him at the library soon as I knew anything. He'd come if we needed him.

I skipped breakfast and hopped on my bike. A heavy gray sky hung close overhead with thunder rumbling around like a giant bass drum.

I made the two miles to Cat's in under ten minutes. She was standing in the open barn loft doors, thirty feet above my head, anxiously beckoning. I flew up the ladder and into The Casbah. The ugly fish lamp was turned up high and the radio was playing a rock tune I didn't recognize.

Lightning crashed in the distance and rain began to dance on the roof. Cat closed the loft doors and pulled some papers from a back pocket of her jeans. She came toward me, holding out the papers, hand trembling, face scrunched into a tense grimace.

"I found these," she said. A tear welled along the edge of her eye and spilled over to trace a sad path down her cheek.

I took the papers, eased her down to a hay bale seat, and put an arm around her soft shoulders. "I love you," I said. "Whatever this is, we'll get through it."

She looked up at me and tried to smile. Another tear slid down the side of her nose. Right then I was so mad at Goody I could have helped do him in, for all the pain he'd caused.

But I kept my mouth shut and turned to the papers Cat gave me. Scrawly handwriting on three sheets of notebook paper. Two pages of notes on ketamine hydrochloride, including how much to take and what to expect. One paragraph was obviously taken from a first hand experience with the drug.

> *Last night I gave myself an intramuscular injection of 100 mg ketamine. I lay down, and within two or three minutes began to experience a contraction of reality that grew until the outside world and my physical body were utterly gone. Then I found myself floating in the midst of a vast vaulted chamber. There was a sense of presence all around, as though I was surrounded by millions of others, although no one else could be seen. In the center of the chamber was a huge, pulsing pyramid of seething energy. I had the feeling that I had stumbled onto the engine that drives the process of creating reality from the thoughts of God. I felt as if I was seeing the truth that thought manifests form, and matter is nothing more than a sonic vibration. And then I was flying over mountain peaks in an unearthly landscape, followed by quick glimpses into other incarnations, other lives I've led, darting journeys through seas of pure information. Then, suddenly, I was back in my body, lying on my bed. Wow, I thought, The ultimate spiritual experience.*

I looked up at Cat. "Jeez," I said. "The same kind of bizarre stuff Pop's French monk was saying. Goody must think he's finally found the magic potion."

Lightning crashed into something close by and Cat jumped. Her lower lip was trembling and it took her a minute to get herself together.

"Read the other page," she said.

> *"Dear Sis,"* Goody wrote in his scrawly hand. *"If this stuff does what they say, I think my search is finally over. Once you've seen the other side there doesn't seem to be much point to this one."*

Another lightning strike rattled the rafters and thunderclaps boomed over our heads, stamping an exclamation to Goody's words.

"I think I might know where he is," Cat said, her voice shaky. "There's an old mine shaft a couple of miles up the gulch below the field behind the barn. It's one of his favorite places."

I reached out my hand to her. A blast of wind shook the barn. Rain crashed against the doors like God's pressure hose at full blast. Lightning cracked so close that I jumped and almost let go Cat's hand. She looked like a wreck about to happen.

I had to shout over the ear bruising thunder that now seemed to come from all directions at once. "Maybe we should move down below," I said. "We're too close to the storm up here with nothing but a few boards between us and............"

A crackling blue flame struck at the socket where the radio plugged in, sizzled a second then streaked up the cord. The radio exploded in a blast of yellowish-blue............then the world stopped.

Slowly, I roused to a fit of violent coughing as heaving lungs pumped air back into sluggish flesh. My body felt like rubber as I struggled to raise my head and will my eyes to focus. I tried to sit up but couldn't do it, fell back onto a hay bale and drifted along the edge of gray consciousness.

After a time, strength began slowly seeping back into trembling muscles. My mind raced like bats through a fog, searching for the will to prod my body into action.

Cat lay crumpled on the dusty floor, a limp scarecrow with ragged breath whistling through slack lips the color of pale orchid.

Part of me screamed to reject this nightmare, to run as fast as I could for the safety of home and wait for morning to chase away the madness. But will won out over the screeching banshees in my head, pushing me forward.

I dragged myself down the ladder, out into the lashing rain, up the drive, into the house, and across the kitchen to the phone.

TWELVE

The next part of that nightmare morning is still blurry, even though my imagination has since tried to fill in some of the blanks. I do remember that by the time the emergency room folks got Cat stabilized, I was functioning pretty well physically, but my brain was like a slow train chugging up a long grade, fighting the job it had to do.

I sat by the bed, holding Cat's cool hand, watching the machines work her body, but her spirit was off somewhere I couldn't reach. Pop sat on the other side of the bed, his head bowed, mouth moving in silent prayer.

I knew we should try to find Goody, but my spirit was weak, and I had trouble finding the energy to move.

Pop was stronger. "We can't do much here but mope and hope," he said. "I think we'd feel better if we were out looking for Christian."

I knew he was right, but it still took almost all I had to drag myself away from Cat.

We found the gulch all right. The old road winding through it was pretty rocky and made for wagons not pickups, but it wasn't the first old mining road Pop's pickup had been on. It took a good hour of slow winding around and scouring the hillsides before we finally pulled up at the base of a steep slope where a plume of yellow mine tailings spilled down a rocky grade.

I grabbed the flashlight from the glove box and we started up. Several minutes of scrambling over scrub and boulders brought us to an old shaft that cut into the rock.

The musty tunnel went straight for about thirty yards so there was enough light to see until it made a right angle and turned black as tar, except for a faint red glow about fifty feet in.

I flipped on the flashlight and there was Goody, stretched out on a blanket next to a mound of smoky embers, glassy eyes staring back at us. As we got closer I spied what I was so hoping we wouldn't. An empty syringe lay on the blanket near his outstretched arm, a green-labeled bottle on its side nearby.

I grabbed him by the back of his shirt and shook until I ran out of steam. "You jerk," I yelled. "Everybody else has to suffer for your stupid selfishness."

I was shaking all over. Cat in the hospital, maybe at death's door, and here we were traipsing after this foolish kid who insisted on chasing rainbows and everybody else be damned. *Even the dumbest animals are smarter than some people*, I thought.

Pop put a gentling hand on my arm. "It's no use," he said. "He's so stoned he doesn't know who he is."

It was like lifting a feed sack full of wet clothes, but we eventually dragged him up and out into the fresh air. We sat him down on the ground where he leered like the Cheshire Cat then rolled over on his side and conked out.

We sat for an hour in silence waiting for Goody to sober up enough to help us get him back to the truck. By the time we got to the house, he was able to stumble to the bedroom where he collapsed across the bed.

"That's the downside of a death experience," Pop said in his gentle voice. "Some can't adjust to ordinary living anymore. I suspect the only permanent cure is to make a conscious choice to live."

"Isn't there some medicine for things like this?" I said.

"Medicines and treatments only work if a person wants to get better," Pop said.

"Then we have to find a way to make him want to get better," I said. "For Cat's sake, if not for his."

I could tell Pop was really upset by the way his jaw bunched into a little knot. "I don't know that we can take that responsibility," he said. "Seems to me psychotherapy is the best choice."

"You mean like a psychiatrist?" I said. "They tried that in California. Cat said he was better for awhile, but now look."

"Sometimes it takes years," Pop said. "And sometimes it means an institution for a time."

"What if we don't have years?" I said. "He seems pretty determined."

Pop shook his head. "Maybe if he was willing to listen, but I don't think so," he said. "I think we better get him into a hospital ASAP."

"He seemed willing to listen to you last week," I said.

Pop scratched the back of his head. "It's really up to their guardian, anyway," he said."

"She's not reliable, either," I said. "They don't even know for sure where she is. Anyway, she'd probably think it was us who was crazy if we said Goody was trying to kill himself."

We had been tiptoeing around it, but once the words were out, the reality shocked us into silence.

Pop was the first to recover. "I guess we could try The Truth," he said. "It can be pretty powerful sometimes. But right now I think prayer's in order."

We joined hands and Pop lowered his head. "Close your eyes," he said. "Take a deep breath and let it out slowly. Try to clear your mind completely so only the thoughts we invite are allowed."

Four eyes closed. Two pairs of lungs took in all they could hold, and blew it slowly back out.

"Knowing that nothing is impossible to those who believe it so," Pop prayed, "We are asking for guidance to find the way to change Christian Terwilliger's mind from darkness to light. We ask for help to make him understand that he is a spiritual being seeking human experience, not a human being seeking spiritual experience. And we ask for the wisdom to show him that it is absolutely essential to The Grand Plan that he fulfill his time in this realm before passing naturally to the other."

Someone had to stay with Goody, so Pop volunteered. That left me free to get back to the hospital and wait for Cat to wake up. And that's where I spent the rest of the day and night.

THIRTEEN

It was a long bleak night by Cat's bed with almost no sleep. But the strange part was, I didn't feel especially tired. Just drained, empty, running on fumes.

Pop called just after daylight. He was anxious to know how Cat was. I told him what they kept telling me: that she wasn't any worse, as if that was supposed to make us feel better.

"I made a big mistake," he said. I could hear the tension in his voice. "Goody seemed fine this morning. Like nothing ever happened. He asked about Carole Ann, and I told him. I shouldn't have. He's barricaded himself in the barn loft. I think you'd better come."

I cursed Goody every step of the six blocks across town. I found Pop in the barnyard shielding his eyes with a hand and looking up at the hayloft doors which were wide open, thirty feet above his head. Goody stood in the opening, leaning out over the edge, looking up toward the sky.

"Hey, Goody," I called.

Goody looked down, glassy-eyed and confused for a moment, then seemed to find himself. "Hey Tom," he said.

"Whatcha doin' up there?" I said.

Goody didn't seem to register the question, just lifted his head back toward the brilliant sky.

"Christian," Pop said. "Come down, I need to talk to you."

Goody looked down at Pop like he hadn't noticed him. Then he shook his head. "Can't do it," he said.

"Wait just a minute, I have something to tell you," Pop said.

Goody's feet scuffed closer to the edge of the opening, "What do you want?" he said.

"I want to tell you a story," Pop said.

Goody looked out at the tops of the cottonwoods around the barn while he weighed this information.

"It's a good story, with a happy ending," Pop began, looking up at Goody and shading his eyes from the morning sun. "It won't take long. If you don't like it you can stop me anytime."

By this time Goody had his toes poking over the edge of the loft floor. He took another look at the treetops then leaned farther out the opening and peered down at us. I thought he was going to do a swan dive right then, and I started easing forward, hoping to somehow cushion his fall.

Pop pointed a rigid finger at Goody's head. "Stop right there," he barked. "Just listen for a minute.

"Long ago in a far away land, there lived a clever youth who became obsessed with wondering where he came from. He believed that the world worked too well for it to be an accident, so he spent a long time thinking about possibilities, and decided there had to be intelligent thought behind it somewhere. The more he pondered, the more it made sense that it all had to start with an idea like everything does, a thought from somewhere. He rejected the stories of an old man in the sky who created the world in seven days. The old man would have had to come from some place. So, he came to believe that the world he knew had to start with a thought. But where did the thought come from? Since there was no world yet, it had to originate somewhere else. That meant there had to be a thought place that he couldn't see or feel, a place where everything, including ourselves, is thought into existence. If this were true, as it seemed to be, then it must also take continuous thought from the thought place to keep everything functioning.

"So, he came to the conclusion that everything we know, including ourselves, had to be a thought that existed in two places at the same time, one place we could see, the other we couldn't. And since thought originated in the thought world and projected into this world, it meant the world we believe is so real had to be an illusion. The thought world had to be the true world, because everything originated there.

"Reason had brought the understanding that thought energy from an unseen place created the world we know, and kept it going with continual thought support.

"The boy decided he had deciphered the mystery of life. He named the invisible thought originator the One Mind, and began to think of it as OM."

Pop paused, eyes shaded, studying Goody's face. Goody's toes were still hooked over the edge of the loft floor, but Pop had his attention for the moment at least.

"But one day the boy woke up," Pop continued, "And realized there was more to the question than just the existence of OM—Why did OM think us into being? What are we here for? The boy was discouraged. The answer to one mystery only led to another.

"After a time he put aside his frustration and began to ponder again. Why would OM thought-create the world in the first place? Hmmm. OM-thought is invisible, but our world is visible. Maybe our world is necessary for transforming invisible thought into visible action. Then it came to him as clear as spring water on a summer day. The process must be like a stage play, where it takes three elements for the story to come to life. The author, that's OM, to conceive the story and the setting. The actors and the scenery, that's our world and all in it, to portray the story. And the audience, which in this case can only be OM again, to experience the story. Without any one of these three, the life we know would not exist. And if the purpose of a stage play is for the audience to experience it, then the purpose of life must be for OM to experience it. Otherwise, OM could only imagine what experiences might be like, and we all know that's not the same as the real thing.

"So, it must be that OM conceived the world, thought-created everything we know from Its own undifferentiated energy, and became the world and everything in it, like an actor puts on a costume and becomes a character in a play. Then OM sat back and experienced The Grand Pageant It had created, actually experiencing Itself through our visible world.

"The boy was very pleased that the answers to life's great mysteries had finally been revealed to him. He lay down to rest from his mental labors. But as soon as his head hit the pillow he bolted upright and groaned. He realized there was yet a third mystery that had not been solved—what happens when something in our world dies?"

Pop paused again, eyeing Goody who was now holding onto one of the pushed back loft doors, zeroed in on Pop like there was nothing else in the Universe.

Pop took a breath and picked up where he'd left off. "So the boy's mind went back to work, turning over and over the ultimate mystery of death. Since he now believed that OM's continuous thought support is required to sustain life, then the only possible explanation for death had to be that the thought support was withdrawn for some reason. Could it be that the character in the pageant had fulfilled its role, providing the experience required of it, and was no longer needed? Yes, that had to be the answer. When the character in the play is no longer necessary to the story, or when a scene ends, the actor sheds the character like a cast-off costume. Then what happens to the character? No, it doesn't cease to exist; it's just no longer visible. It is still very much alive and well, in the mind of the audience. And the audience for The Grand Pageant of Life is OM, where the character originated. Aha! The hope we have of ourselves as somehow immortal was true, though it may not be in the form some would like to believe.

"The boy was very pleased. All the great mysteries seemed to be solved. What am I, and where do I come from? I am a visible manifestation of The One Pure Thought Energy Source, OM, originated and maintained by OM-thought.

"What am I doing here, and what purpose do I serve? I serve as a physical medium for OM to experience Itself as Life.

"Why do I die, and what happens to me after? I die when my role has been completed or when my character is no longer necessary in The Grand Pageant of Life. After OM withdraws my life supporting thought, I continue to exist eternally as a thought-image in the very real but unseen Universal Mind of OM.

"The boy rejoiced in his knowledge, satisfied that he now had all the answers he needed to fulfill his role in life.

"But he woke one morning again in despair, realizing there was one final missing piece to the puzzle."

Pop paused again, though he didn't need to worry about Goody for the moment. We were both hanging on every word, even me though I'd heard it all before.

"Does OM have a Grand Plan," Pop continued, "Or does everything happen randomly, for the purpose of the experience only? The boy resumed his ponderous labors, reviewing what he had so far observed in life. Great good fortune sometimes happens. Great catastrophes sometimes happen. Is it all an accident? His mind went back to The Grand Stage Play idea. If that were true, and he believed it so, then the author, OM, thought-creates the play, the stage setting, and the players. The players, which is all of creation including us, are supposed to follow the script. But, OM gave people the ability to think independent thoughts. And like actors in a play, they may decide their way is better, taking off in an independent direction with their own interpretation of the script, creating an entirely different scene than the author envisioned.

"Yes, people did have the power to think independent thoughts. And the boy had already concluded that thought could create things and events. The incredible implication of this reasoning suddenly hit him—***People also have the power to thought-create things and events independent of OM.*** By giving people the ability to thought-create as an extension of Itself, OM could thus experience myriad, random events without actually planning them, and the events could surprise even Itself.

"So it seemed that OM did indeed have a Grand Plan, and it was that our world continue to exist as The Grand Stage upon which is played out The Grand Pageant of Life. And by giving mankind the power of independent thought, OM would only need to intervene in the life process if the survival of The Grand Pageant is threatened.

"The boy gave thanks to OM for the knowledge he had been given. He went back to being an ordinary youth, satisfied he had all the answers he needed to go on with his life, content to play his role, knowing that he was vitally important to the process, even if he didn't yet know what his true purpose was. He could leave that to OM."

Pop was rolling full-speed now, using his voice and his body to give us the Sunday Show, and nobody was thinking about ducking out. There would be no stopping now 'til the tale was finished.

"But the introspective boy grew into a searching man," Pop continued. "He took up the pursuit of knowledge as a drowning person grasps a rope, studying all the great works that human effort had produced. He devoured the known scientific tomes, and absorbed the great philosophers' wisdom. Every step up the ladder of human understanding took him a bit farther from the truths he had divined as a youth. Each scientific fact accepted without question dimmed the brilliant light of youthful insight a bit more. Until one day he looked back on his callow innocence and chuckled at the naïve mind that reasoned the existence of OM.

"The young man idled with his friends in the wine shops and scoffed. 'There was no invisible intelligence creating and guiding the life process,' they sneered. It was all one complex accident dependent only on a few simple scientific laws. Man was a random result of genetic mutations evolving over millennia. We were born, we strove to survive and procreate, and we died, our bodies decomposing into their basic elements, our psyches ceasing to exist for all time. It was only man's colossal ego that drove the compulsion to explain his existence in cosmic terms. A tyrannical ego which cannot accept its own mortality, demanding instead an absurd myth that promises immortality. Man was truly the most pitiful of all creatures, a hapless victim of happenstance, totally alone, born to die and so painfully aware of the knowledge.

"So the young man drank wine and consorted with nubile women. Why should he strive to achieve when all in life was hopeless vanity, doomed to extinction? He sowed his seed in willing fields until one seed took sprout, and the man was coerced into marriage.

"With a heavy heart, he surrendered his freedom and took up the burden of living. A child was born, and the man toiled under the sun to feed his family. Surprising even himself, he found the hard work rewarding and he relaxed in the evening with a flagon of wine. But gradually, he became aware of a smoldering ember of unnamed fear in his breast, like summer lightning just over the horizon. A flagon of wine helped to soothe the threatening storm.

"Then misfortune intervened. The crop failed. His son sickened and died. His wife grew shrewish and spat blame upon him. The man cursed his humanity and drank more wine to dull the pain.

"Misfortune ran its course. The next crop was bountiful. His wife warmed again to his touch. Another son was born. His family prospered. He celebrated his good fortune with more wine. It no longer mattered whether he was immortal or not. Life was sufficient unto itself. Sometimes he could even forget the kernel of dread that pulsed deep within him.

"Years passed. His family increased. The rains came, the sun shone, his fields produced crop after prosperous crop and he continued to celebrate his good fortune with more and better wines. But in the dark of night he felt the festering unnamed fear, churning, threatening.

"He began to have dark dreams, waking in the morning to consuming tremors of impending doom. So each night he drank yet more wine, hoping to quiet the fears as before. But, instead, the dreams grew worse, and the fears throbbed.

"Then the rains stopped. The crops withered under a blistering sun. His children grew ill in the night, and one by one were buried along side his firstborn son. His wife wailed and took to her bed, refusing to eat. Despair consumed him. Each night he sought the wine bottle like a newborn seeks the nipple. And the demons came, driving away sleep, forcing him from the bed to stagger out into the darkness where the twinkling sky mocked his pitiful insignificance.

"Hopelessness overwhelmed him. He cursed the stars, he cursed the ground, he railed in despair at his helplessness. He took the knife from his belt, held it high in his fist and plunged it into his chest. The blade struck a rib, slid along his side, and flew from his hand. He crumpled into the dust, and surrendered to oblivion.

"His mind drifted for a time, empty and formless. Then he seemed to be floating, womb-like, suspended in an invisible sea, caressed by unseen waves of soothing delight. Like floating on a fragrant summer breeze. Slowly he became aware that he wasn't floating on the breeze at all. He was the breeze. Dissolved into it like water dripped into a stream. Instead of flowing *around* him, the caressing wave flowed *through* him, caring, nourishing, sustaining.

"Suddenly, he began to feel a tingling in the wave, like a tiny current through a hair-like filament. The exquisite tingling grew, coursing through his being, surging and waning in nanosecond tides. After a time, it seemed the tingling became a murmur, like a soft string plucked and dampered, and he strained to make it out. But then he realized it wasn't sound he was sensing, it was the wave itself, bathing every part of his being, changing his body from solid mass to shimmering light. The wave continued to flow, melding itself with his essence, awakening indescribable sensations, infusing all knowledge, quickening a joy beyond telling.

"He drifted, no longer individual, but now one with an absolute universe. Pure energy essence dissolved in the One Mind that is All. Peace, joy, serenity, and awareness beyond human comprehension.

"Slowly, caressing waves of infinite wisdom began to seep into his awareness, forming misty thoughts that swirled into fuzzy letters, then finally into words like vapor trails in a cloudless sky:

> *We Are One. Infinite and Eternal. All Creation Flows From Us. Through Our Thoughts. Manifesting According to Our Expectations. As We Think, So We Are. Know This and Create Abundance.*

"Then sudden, engulfing certainty that he must return to the fantasy world of human experience to fulfill the role assigned from the beginning. Then the wrench of excruciating rending from the oneness with All, in bloody separation of rebirth.

"The night passed. The morning sun rose in brilliant promise. The man woke joyful, refreshed, and went into the house to share the 'Dream' with his wife. When he finished his tale, she got up from the bed and began to dress his wound.

"He resumed his life, sharing the secret of his 'Dream' with all who came his way. He took up his tools and toiled joyfully in his fields from morning 'til dusk. At the end of each day he recalled the 'Dream' and gave thanks to OM.

"Soon, he realized the dreadful fears had vanished, and he no longer sought solace from a wine bottle. He reveled in this new-found freedom. His holdings once again prospered, his wife brought forth new life, and he rejoiced.

"And so, he passed his days in joyous labor and gratitude for the opportunity to serve his purpose, content in the certainty that he would one day return to the place of his 'Dream'. When his children were of age, he took them aside and taught them the wonderful Truth he had been given.

"He lived to bury his beloved wife, saddened, but secure in the knowledge that they would one day be reunited in OM. Finally, the day came when he woke to the welcome awareness that his time was near, and he lay back in his bed. His family gathered around him and began weeping. He summoned his failing strength and said to them:

> *Do not weep, for the blessed time is near. Rejoice for my sake, and remember these things I have taught you. In the beginning there was only the One Mind of pure thought energy, OM. Like an author creates scenes to bring his thoughts to life, OM thought-created us and our world into existence, and continuously thought-sustains it. Through us and our thought-created world, OM can experience life events rather than just imagining them. Each of us as players has a crucial role in the play, though we may not clearly see it. We fulfill that role by expressing OM thought-energy*

through our minds, creating life according to our beliefs.
When our role is finished, we are free to exit the scene, to be
immortalized in the mind energy of the audience, OM. OM,
the One Mind, is us, we are It. We can never be separated.

That said, and with a smile on his lips, the old man closed his eyes and breathed his last. OM was waiting.

By the time Pop finished his story, Goody was sitting down on the loft floor, his feet dangling out the doorway. No one spoke for a long time.

Even from a distance I could see Goody's eyes were wet as he looked down at Pop. "Where'd you get that story?" he said.

"Pop made it up," I said.

Goody looked at Pop like he'd just dropped out of the sky.

Pop smiled and held out his arms. "We each have an important role to play, even if it's not absolutely clear to us," he said. "But the future truly is ours to shape. It can literally be anything we want it to be. Nothing is impossible. We only have to choose what it is we wish to experience and believe in our creative power. Come on down and let's go see to your sister."

Goody wobbled to his feet. Then turned and started down the ladder.

FOURTEEN

I was the first one into Cat's hospital room, my heart fluttering like a moth at a flame. A nurse was unhooking monitor leads from Cat's chest, the breathing machine a silent sentry beside the bed. Cat's hair spread like a copper hemorrhage around her marble face, lily-like hands folded across the sheet that covered her legs.

The nurse jerked back from Cat when she saw us. "Oh, Jesus," she said. "I'll get the doctor."

My legs turned to Jell-O and I slumped into a chair by the bed. My throat started to choke and I couldn't catch my breath.

Goody stood stiff as a post on the other side of the bed, looking down at Cat's still form, his face like granite. Then slowly the granite began to crumble. A tremble started in his chin, and spread upward to his lower lip. His hands flew up to cover his face. He threw himself onto the bed, his body quaking like aspen in a windstorm.

Pop bent down, folded Goody against his chest, and held on while Goody's body convulsed in shuddering sobs.

Slowly I realized I wasn't breathing. I was surprised to find my heart still beating. I took in a great gasp of air, and my chest began pumping like a windmill loosed from its tethering chain.

The doctor burst in, the flustered nurse at his heels. "We tried to reach you," he said. "Her heart just quit. We did all we could to resuscitate, but got no response. I'm sorry."

I couldn't speak. My mouth wouldn't work.

"Thank you," Pop said. "Could we have a few minutes alone?"

"As long as you need," the doctor said.

"If you would just push the call button when you're ready," the nurse said.

I sat and stared at Cat's exquisite face. Her hair was like a brilliant halo against the stark pillow. The freckles across her nose stood out more clearly than ever but the rose spots on her cheeks were gone, replaced by cool alabaster. Her once poppy-like lips now pale orchid. I took her hand. It was soft and dry, like a fine doeskin glove.

I could feel my heart beating now, my chest breathing, my fingers and toes all in place. But something was missing inside. I felt like a shadow, my spirit bled away in the wake of her passage.

Goody looked up from across the bed, eyes like dripping coals, face etched in anguish, streaked with tear-tracks. He held Cat's other lifeless hand in both of his. A sudden spasm shook his frame, his face bunched into a wretched knot, his mouth stretched in a tortured *O*.

Pop straightened and held out his hands to Goody and me. "Close the circle," he said.

We joined hands. Goody to Cat to me to Pop to Goody.

"Omniscient OM," Pop prayed, softly. "We cry out in anguish for the loss of Carole Ann Terwilliger. Even though we know she still lives in your realm, we can't imagine how we can continue without her in ours. We are blinded by grief and fear, and do not understand the loss of one so young and vibrant."

Pop's voice rose like a Baptist preacher at a Missouri revival. "We pray that Carole Ann's accident was a random event, and the death of her body a reversible error. With all our being we place our trust in your Truth which tells us that not only your thoughts, but also our thoughts, have infinite power to change our physical world. In our agony we claim this birthright and manifest Carole Ann as restored to us."

A wave of fear ran up my spine, and the hair on the back of my neck jumped to attention. Pop was praying to raise Cat from the dead.

A second later, a tiny current rippled into the hand Pop was holding, ran up my arm, across my shoulders, down the other arm, and into the hand that held Cat's. My imagination thought it felt a flicker of warmth as the current passed into Cat's hand. But an instant later the hand I held was once again cool doeskin.

Pop's hand relaxed in mine and Goody began to sob again, but more softly now. We sat like that for a long time. My mind careened around in a hopeless search for painless oblivion. Gradually, Goody quieted and the silence closed in around us.

Our hands slipped apart. Pop reached for the call button above the bed. The nurse came and pulled the sheet over Cat's head.

And my life was over.

FIFTEEN

Pop, Goody and I dragged ourselves back to the ranch. We slumped into the house and sat in stunned silence, broken only by occasional choking sobs from first one then another.

My body was numb, but my mind was churning a fragmented stew of tortured pain. How could God let this happen? Why not me? Why hadn't the rest of the world stopped? How could the sun keep on shining? Where was she? It seemed like the devil's fire raged through my brain, destroying all hope of peace forever as I wallowed in the hellish depths of despair.

I guess a long time passed, but I don't know. When I finally looked up, Goody sat with his face buried in his hands, once in a while shaking his head and moving a hand to wipe his nose. Pop stared straight ahead, eyes wet, jaw muscles bunched into knots, rocking slowly back and forth.

Pop leaned forward and held out his hands to us. "We have to try to pray," he said.

Goody dropped his hands and gaped at Pop, his eyes tormented fires. "You almost had me believing all that bullshit," he said. "Pray to what? For what? How can you still believe in a caring God that supposedly looks out for his helpless children?"

Pop winced, but extended his hand. "Prayer isn't always to an omnipotent power," he said. "Some believe prayer is actually a way of focusing our own power to alter our circumstances, or heal our pain. And two or more together in prayer increase the power exponentially. Help us, please."

Goody shook his head and sighed, but stretched out his hands toward us. Six hands joined in a circle. Pop bowed his head and opened his mouth to begin.

Then the most incredible thing I've ever seen began. Goody started to speak. Softly, almost mumbling at first, so I had to strain to hear. Then building in volume, his words like a current shocking our minds.

Hey. It's okay. I'm here and it's just like Goody said.

I know I must have goggled like a slack-jawed fool. Pop's hand tightened on mine in a vise-grip. He was staring at Goody like he was hearing Chinese.

Goody sat like a Buddha, eyes fixed and unblinking. The voice was his own, but there was no mistaking Cat's words as he spoke.

After I felt the lightning slam into me, it was like I was drifting down a warm, silent stream in the blackest night possible.

Goody took a deep breath and continued his unbelievable speech.

Then all of a sudden, I was in this perfect place like nothing you've ever felt. Just this total loving, peaceful light that swirled all around and through me. And I knew. This was the place Pop and Goody talked about. The thought place we come from and go back to, where we're not separate and apart anymore. Where everything is peace and love, and we're part of it.

Even now as I remember back on that incredible scene, my mind wants to reject the picture of Goody sitting like a statue on our old couch, channeling Cat's voice as if it was the most normal thing in the world. I know what I heard, but to this day it's still hard to believe.

Then I realized I wasn't just a drop in a sea of love-light, Goody/Cat was saying. I saw that part of me was still a body in an Arizona hospital bed. I watched you all sitting around the bed as I floated above. It was really weird because I remembered being in that body but I couldn't feel it any more. It was like watching an old home movie of people you once knew so well but who are now just hazy memories in a poignant past. As I floated, part of me merged with the perfect place, another part of me was drawn to that sad form on the bed below.

The next thing I knew I was jerked from the love-place and woke up back in the body of Carole Ann Terwilliger.

And that's where I am. Come and see.

Goody yanked his hands free from ours and shook himself like a dog after a bath. His eyes were wide, his mouth slack.

"Oh, my," Pop said to Goody. "Do you remember any of that?"

Goody's lips worked, but he couldn't seem to find his voice.

"You were Cat," I said. "She was talking to us through you. She......." I ran out of words.

"She talked to us from the other side," Pop said. "She said she was back....alive."

Goody's eyes were still glassy but he managed a whisper. "I…..I sort of remember," he said. "Like a…..like a dream when you just wake up."

I looked at Pop. "Can it be true?" I said. "I can't handle anymore grief."

The phone rang, jarring us back to reality. Pop picked it up.

"Yes," he said, his face a blank mask as he listened. "Thank you."

He put down the phone and took us both into his gaze. "That was Carole Anne's doctor. He said they're required to check for life signs one last time before pronouncing death. And someone thought they felt a tiny pulse, so they went back to work on her. He doesn't understand, but she is resuscitated and breathing on her own."

"Oh my God," Goody said.

"Exactly," Pop said.

I don't recall Pop driving us to the hospital, though he told me later he broke every traffic rule. But I will never forget the three of us hovering over Cat's bed, watching the gentle rise and fall of the sheet as she quietly breathed. And don't ever try to tell me there's no such thing as a miracle. Because I was there, I lived it. I saw the roses returned to her cheeks and the pink once again tinting her delicious lips. And I remember the indescribable joy when her eyelids fluttered up, and her hand found mine resting on the sheet.

And I will forever recall the thrill that ran up my spine when she smiled into my eyes and said, "Hi".

SIXTEEN

I was startled from my reverie when the door to Pop's hospital room creaked opened. My wife tiptoed in, her swelling belly like a growing melon preparing for harvest. She came to me, smiling, bent and kissed my face. Her copper hair tickled my cheek.

"How is he?" she said.

"Not good," I said. "Comatose." I patted her belly. "How are you?"

"Pooped," she said. "But it's been rougher on you, I think."

I squeezed her hand. "It's better now," I said.

She leaned onto my chest and I folded her into my arms. Her shoulders shook with silent little sobs that drowned themselves in the cloth of my shirt. Pop used to say she was so tender hearted he didn't know how she managed to cope in this sometimes-heartless world. But I know. Underneath that doeskin façade there's a knowing toughness that always shows through in the clenches. She's found that tiny kernel of eternal serenity, the secret place within that knows who she really is, that no matter what is raging, nothing can really harm us. Cat Ripley is one truly extraordinary person, and I am so welded to her essence I doubt a cutting torch could sever the bond.

"I brought my brother back," Cat said.

"Where is he?" I said.

"Out in the hall," she said. "We weren't sure...."

I went to the door and poked my head out. "Hey, get in here," I said.

He stuck out his hand. I took it, folded him into a hug, then held him at arm's length. His black eyes were moist.

"Good old Tom," he said.

"Goody," I said. "But, I guess it's Reverend Terwilliger now. Congratulations."

"I'm still just Goody," he said. "Wearing a different hat, that's all. Did Cat tell you I've been offered Unity Church?"

"Namaste," I said. The family was coming back together again.

We gathered around Pop's bed. Goody took one of the wrinkled hands in his own. Cat stroked Pop's hair and bent to kiss his forehead.

Pop's eyes snapped open. A tear rolled down the deep furrow in his cheek. His lips parted. In a shaky, halting voice, but as clear as ever, he said:

Th..Thank...God. My..three...kids.

Unbelievable. No trace of stroke damaged speech.

"We love you, Pop," Cat said.

Not..much...time, Pop said. Amazing.

"Take it easy, Pop," I said. "No need to talk."

Must..remind...you, he said. He took a shallow breath and raised a trembling hand.... *We're. Just. Imaginary...Sojourners. In...a...Fantasy. World. Our time...here....short. Our...True...Home...Unity...With...The...One..Mind.*

His voice faltered. He rested a moment and started again. *We..have.. power...to..to create...painful struggle...or joyous....adventure. Pain..from...ignorance. Joy..from...Truth. Always. Remember. Who..who.. You. Are. And....live....the..joyous. Truth......of...Oneness. With. OM.*

He gave us a last, weak smile, then slid back into unconsciousness.

We buried Pop in the old Elk's Cemetery, on a rocky slope that overlooks town. In time we found the right words for the granite slab marking his grave.

Late on a brilliant afternoon in the fall of 1990, four of us went up the hill to see the new marker. I pulled a few weeds and brushed dirt from the fresh concrete base. Cat put her free arm around my waist. Goody held baby Andy. I took a moment to wipe my nose. Then read from the stone:

Father Andrew Ripley
Pop
Dec. 15, 1915–Sept. 28, 1990
With OM.

We stayed until the afternoon shadows crept through the cedars, savoring the rocky simplicity of the cemetery, the crisp air, the perfect sky, the pine-covered mountains rolling into the distant haze.

Then it was time for evening chores. The livestock were waiting. We went back down the hill, and headed home to the ranch.

0-595-32457-6

Printed in the United States
21404LVS00001B/55-102